Praise for *Mirror, Mirror*

"Edgerton is one of the best writers around for inventing dire dilemmas for his protagonists, and here he's at his best because he's created a paranormal environment where he's not bound by laws of physics, time, or space. Turn Les loose like that and you're in for a scary ride."
—Carl R. Brush, author of *The Second Vendetta*

"Fantastic! Fast-paced and written in Edgerton's distinctive, take-no-prisoners-style. I'm not your usual YA fan, but this was right up my alley."
—Maegan Beaumont, author of the Sabrina Vaughn novels

"This is Les Edgerton's only YA book, and it's a great one. It reminds me a little of some old-school *Twilight Zone* tales, in that Edgerton starts with an original premise and then executes it with precision and thoughtfulness. He keeps the tension bouncing along nicely, too."
—Rob Boley, author of the Scary Tales books

Praise for Les Edgerton's Books

"Les Edgerton has swiftly become my favorite crime writer. Original voice, uncompromising attitude and a pure hard-boiled style leap him to the front ranks of my reading list. He will become legendary."
—Joe R. Lansdale, bestselling author

"Les Edgerton brings to this short story collection an unerring ear for dialogue and a sure-handed sense of place (particularly New Orleans, where many of the stories are set). In the best story, 'My Idea of a Nice Thing,' a woman named Raye tells us why she drinks: 'My job. I'm a hairdresser. See, you take on all of these other people's personalities and troubles and things, ten or twelve of 'em a day, and when the end of the day comes, you don't know who you are anymore. It takes three drinks just to sort yourself out again.' Here Edgerton grants both the reader and Raye the grace of irony, and without his authorial intrusion, we find ourselves caring about her predicament."
— *The New York Times Book Review*

"Les Edgerton is the new High King of Noir."
—Ken Bruen, bestselling author

"Edgerton is much more than a fiction writer or a story teller. When you read his work, your ears prick up, your eyes go wide, and your spine tingles. You get the sense that Edgerton has been there, lived the lives of his characters, fought their fights, cried their tears, placed their bets, drank their Wild Turkey, smoked their cigarettes. He writes with a stunning accuracy, a convincing authority and a stark reality. At the same time, he strikes a balance between beauty, sensitivity and humor. Edgerton is not just another stunning narrative talent, he is an important narrative authority—a master of his or any other generation."
—Vincent Zandri, author
of *The Sins of the Sons*

"A Hillbilly Elegy with a deep, pulsing heart, *Adrenaline Junkie* makes sense of one man's life while showing us all new aspects of our own."

—Jenny Milchman, *USA Today* bestselling
and Mary Higgins Clark Award-winning author

"*The Genuine, Imitation, Plastic Kidnapping* is a dark crime comedy that will have you laughing from page one. It crackles with manic energy and mad thrills. If you're looking for a different kind of edgy crime novel, this is the one to grab."

—Bill Crider, author of
the Sheriff Dan Rhodes mysteries

"Masquerading as a novel, Les Edgerton's newest gem— *The Genuine, Imitation, Plastic Kidnapping*—is really a debauched weekend in steamy New Orleans, loaded with alcohol, drugs, whores, pistols, and a menacing bookie, all available for your personal and private entertainment between the covers. Narrator Pete Halliday— ex-con, gambler, boozer, ex-baseball pitcher and unwise wiseass—takes us places most don't really want to go, only to have the time of our lives when we get there."

—Jack Getze, author of
the Austin Carr mysteries

"No one can accuse Les of being a 'crime tourist.' He's lived the life, done the bird, and now he's written the book. *Adrenaline Junkie* should be on any prospective (or established) crime writer's list. An entertaining, darkly-rendered tale of one man's adventures in the very belly of the beast."

—Tony Black, author of *Her Cold Eyes*

"*Adrenaline Junkie* is a raw and harrowing memoir that brilliantly combines great sensitivity with brutal honesty. Les Edgerton is never afraid to reveal his vulnerability—and culpability—as he takes us on a head-spinning ride through the bizarre and terrifying experiences in a life that was often defined by violence. The result is a breath-taking page-turner that will keep readers hooked from page one and will never let them go."

—Lisa Lieberman Doctor, former
Warner Bros. prodco president, president of
Robin Williams prodco, Blue Wolf Productions

"Filled with stories of knifings, armed robberies, brutal prison fights, and Charles Manson (yes, that Charles Manson!), Edgerton proves that life can be stranger (and certainly more violent) than fiction. But Edgerton isn't just a guy with a tough story to tell. He's a poet who startles you with sentences both stark and darkly beautiful. An astonishing accomplishment."

—Jon Bassoff, author of *Corrosion*

"There's nothing fake about *The Genuine, Imitation, Plastic Kidnapping.* Les Edgerton's latest book is the real deal, and has everything to keep you turning the pages. It's a caper, full of fun and high-jinx, but it's also bitter-sweet, engendering a full range of emotions. You'll smile, you'll wince, you'll laugh out loud, and sometimes you'll even cringe, but you'll come away from the read feeling thoroughly satisfied and entertained. A terrific read."

—Matt Hilton, author of
the best-selling Joe Hunter thrillers

MIRROR,
MIRROR

ALSO BY LES EDGERTON

Memoir
Adrenaline Junkie

Novels
The Genuine, Imitation, Plastic Kidnapping
The Rapist
The Bitch
Just Like That
Bomb! (formerly *The Perfect Crime*)
The Death of Tarpons

Short Story Collections
Monday's Meal
Lagniappe

Writer's How-to Craft Books
Finding Your Voice
Hooked

Sports Books
Surviving Little League (co-authored with son Mike when he was twelve)
Perfect Game USA and the Future of Baseball

Other books on business, hairstyling, etc.

LES EDGERTON

MIRROR, MIRROR

DOWN&OUT
BOOKS

Down & Out Books
3959 Van Dyke Rd, Ste. 265
Lutz, FL 33558
www.DownAndOutBooks.com

Cover design by JT Lindroos

ISBN: 1-948235-77-3
ISBN-13: 978-1-948235-77-8

FOREWORD

I wrote this book many years ago and not to publish it but just as a labor of love for my oldest daughter Britney. She was a voracious reader and I simply wanted to write something just for her that she could look at and say, "My dad wrote this for me." In other words, I wanted her to be proud of me.

When she read it, she turned to me and told me it was the scariest thing she'd ever read. Keep in mind she was about nine years old at the time, so it wasn't as if she'd read thousands of books. But, it made me feel great.

When her little sister Siena came along, both Britney and I urged her to read it. She did and she had much the same reaction as her sister had. Scared the pants off her! I thought for the first time that maybe it might be publishable, but it wasn't until a few years ago when Britney and I were talking about everyday things, when Britney suddenly said, "You know, Dad, after I read *Mirror, Mirror*

I couldn't look into a mirror at myself for more than a few seconds at a time before I had to look away. It just scared the crap out of me!"

And that's when I realized it was publishable. And so, I find myself with the pleasurable task of determining who to dedicate this, my fifteenth book published, and it's a no-brainer. *Mirror, Mirror* is dedicated to both of my little girls who taught me anew that it's the joy of writing that affects another person's emotions that's the real reward of being a writer.

And, upon this reissue, I have a great opportunity to include someone else in this dedication. In the last year, my long-lost daughter, Maria Sherer-Lutz found me with a DNA test and now I have a new daughter!

Thanks, Britney and Sienna and Maria! I love you.

CHAPTER ONE

I'm inside my bathroom mirror.

I don't mean in the cabinet behind the mirror. I mean, *I'm inside my bathroom mirror.*

The *bad* news is, I can't get out.

There isn't what I'd call a lot of good news.

I'm trapped. Forever, if I want to believe Liz.

Liz is my mirror-world counterpart. See, my name is Elizabeth, Elizabeth Mary Downing, and I'm inside this mirror and Liz—she's the original occupant, the one who trapped me in here—is out where I used to be. She's three-dimensional and I'm flat like a Gumby character. It used to be the other way around.

She tricked me.

She had two powerful weapons that she used to get me to trade places with her. Vanity and curiosity. *My* vanity, *my* curiosity.

It's a long story.

And it's still going on...

CHAPTER TWO

It all really started years ago, ten years ago to be exact, when I was six years old. Ever since I can remember I've had this strange feeling whenever I looked into a mirror that there was someone on the other side staring back at me. I mean, someone not myself. Every time I passed a mirror, I swore I saw something that wasn't supposed to be there. What, I couldn't tell you, just something extra in there that didn't belong.

When I was in kindergarten, I had an experience that convinced me this was more than just some wacko dream I'd gotten from standing too close to my mom, inhaling Drano fumes, when she was using it on the sinks. I was in my parents' bedroom, fooling around, "getting into trouble" as my dad likes to say, and I climbed up on the chair that sits in front of their dressing table. Of course, it had a large mirror and, of course, I had to look into it. What kid could resist? At first, all I saw was myself looking back, a girl dressed in the same brown overalls I was wearing, hair the same whitish-blonde as it was then (it's a darker blonde now) and every other detail mine, except for one tiny difference: My eyes are the brown of dead oak trees and the person looking back had gorgeous blue eyes. I swear I'm not making this up! I didn't even notice the discrepancy right away, and if I had been the average six-year-old and not too observant, maybe it would never have dawned on me that the eyes were a different color. But I have always been all too aware of the color of my eyes, having wished long before I was even six for blue ones instead of these mud-colored things I'm stuck with. I saw the difference right away.

I scooted my cute little butt right off that chair and ran screaming into the kitchen where my mom was fixing sandwiches for lunch.

"Mommy!" I screeched. Naturally, my mother thought I had chopped off a finger or something so she checked me all over for blood and broken bones, and when she saw I was in one piece she just laughed while I tried to tell her about the girl in the mirror.

"Mom, there really is. Honest, Mommy, honest." Even my tears didn't help. My mother can be a cold, cold woman sometimes. Joan Crawford's kid was a lucky slob, compared with me.

"Well, of course there is, Elizabeth. Just like there was an alien in your bedroom last night, sitting on the dresser. Now go play and let Mommy get lunch started. Go outside and ride your bike, dear. You need fresh air."

What I needed was a mom who didn't think I suffered from hallucinations.

I'll admit, after a few more tears, she did go into her bedroom and look into the mirror with me, even forcing me to again look into the mirror, at which I did some healthy yelling, but she was right—there was no one there this time, except her and me...and my dumb brown eyes. I stayed mad all that night, refusing to eat anything at supper except my dessert, which was chocolate pudding, my favorite at the time, and I got mad all over again when she told my father about it and he yukked it up.

"Quite the imagination, little princess," he said, reaching over and patting the top of my head. I ducked and gave him my best glare, but all he did was laugh and say, "Here we have the next Steven Spielberg. We'll want to remember this moment when she's rich and famous." I'm frightened out of my wits and all they think is that I have this retarded imagination. Is that fair?

The mirror person never appeared again...until two weeks ago. For years and years she'd stayed away until even *I* began to think I'd imagined the whole deal.

I wish I had imagined it.

CHAPTER THREE

She's baaaa-aack.

Miss Blue Eyes.

In the hall mirror, where I do my last minute face-on-right check. She was the same age as me and dressed identically, which shows, at the very least, extremely good taste on her part. I was on my way out of the door to go to school—my boyfriend, Jimmy French, was tooting his horn like the Doofus of the Month he is sometimes (like on days ending in "y")—and I just peeked into the mirror to see if my hair was okay and if there was anything from breakfast on my teeth, like a piece of egg or something, and lo and behold, there she was again, blue eyes and all.

Oh, boy.

Yow.

Double yow.

I didn't scream this time, but I did jump like I'd

been poked with one of those cattle prods, and I tore out of the house like Freddy Krueger had just peeked in the window. I jumped into Jimmy's car and slid over by him, quick-like, and being the slowhead that he is, ol' Jimmeroo thought I was that glad to see him and not scared out of my Calvin Klein jockeys, which is what I was. For a minute, I thought about clueing him in but decided not to, remembering Mom's response a century before. Jimmy's comments would be a thousand times worse than anything Mom had ever said.

"Whatsa matter?" he said. "You look like you've seen a ghost." Originality is not one of Jimmy's hot traits. I hope he doesn't decide to become a writer. He might make a decent president, though. I've noticed they use clichés like they invented them.

"It's nothing," I said. "*Look out!*" He was bearing into the opposite lane and a bus was coming at us. Jimmy's one of those guys who turns the car in the direction he's looking. I have an uncle like that. Every time he goes to change the radio station and reaches for the dial or pushes the cigarette lighter in he ends up in somebody's front yard. I think he's trying to invent a new way of dying from smoking. It must be a guy thing. You want to keep Jimmy's attention on the road ahead at all times, just like Uncle Rob; otherwise, he ends up on somebody's front yard or standing on his brakes.

I shook all the way to school, my teeth clacking like a set of castanets, and Jimmy dummied up. Mad, at my backseat driving. About a block from school his pout ended and he asked me again what was wrong.

"I'm freezing, hon," I said, and patted his arm. The fact that it was Indian summer and eighty-two degrees Fahrenheit at eight a.m. didn't enter his brain cavity because he just grinned like a game show host and hugged me closer like he thought he was saving me from frostbite. Comfort was what I needed, so I didn't say any more, and by the time we pulled into the school parking lot I was only shaking like an Indiana earthquake, which doesn't do much to Mr. Richter Scale. When we went up the steps I saw a bunch of my friends and we started yakking and screaming like we always do, and I pushed the mirror person to the back closet of my mind for the time being. I waved goodbye to Jimmy and went on into the building with my buds.

Like *hel*-lo. Like I could really forget something like that. Duh.

First period class was all right; it's algebra and you have to use your brain waves to keep up, so I was okay there. But second period is English and we were studying Wordsworth the poet, who I know is this great literary figure and all, but kind of a mood-setter for naps sometimes, too—I mean, why can't we study song lyrics more, like, for instance, the words from Green Day's "Longview"—that's poetry too, isn't it? Unless you're a hundred and thirty-five. Anyway, my mind zoned out on me in English and up popped the mirror girl. Next class

was health and that was the bummiest. I got embarrassed when Mr. Swartz asked me what the chief
cause of drowning was and I said "water" without
thinking. It got a big laugh from everybody except
Mr. Swartz. who just gave this famous frown he's
notorious for, but which doesn't intimidate anybody
except maybe his poor wife, but the bad thing is
now I'll bet you any amount of money he thinks of
me as the class clown or something totally zero like
that, and which I don't need. I have to have a good
grade in his class to get into medical school eventually, which is where Mom and Dad want me to go,
but I think I'd rather be a marine biologist—I mean,
aren't those seals just the cutest things? I'm with
Jane Fonda on this one, even though as an actress I
think Angela what's-her-name from that series "My
So-Called Life" is yards better, but who knows
what Angela thinks about our ocean friends? At
least Jane Fonda puts her money where her mouth
is and I admire her for that.

Already that mirror person was getting me into
trouble!

At noon, all of us girls go into the bathroom to
trade makeup secrets and talk about our boyfriends
and teachers and who's the worst-dressed in school
and who's the best-dressed and then we picture them
out on a date. It's a hoot! Sometimes it gets a little
cruel and I don't like it when that happens; I mean,
those are people, too, but usually it's just in good
fun and nobody gets hurt, unless you call getting a

reputation for being the worst-dressed a harmful thing, which, as I think about it, is, so maybe we shouldn't be doing that. I'll bring it up, see if some of the others think the same.

It'll have to be tomorrow, because I absolutely couldn't enter the bathroom. Do you know how many mirrors there are in the girls' bathroom? Only about a million and a half!

In fact, I never once even looked into my compact to see if my mascara was running or if my cheeks were too pale, because I just knew Blue Eyes would be staring back out at me. I could have had a hunk of Pizza Hut pretend cheese between my teeth and looked like a gomer all day for all I knew, except no one said I did and I know that if I did Missi Smith would have been only too glad to point it out as she thrives on telling you your faults and bad points whenever she can. Not going to the bathroom with my friends caused me all kinds of grief, since now they all think I've got some kind of nose problem and I'm too good for them, which is, of course, ridiculous, but I certainly can't tell them the real reason I didn't go to the bathroom. My kidneys must look like one of those water balloons stretched out. I'm developing a serious phobia about mirrors. I'll have to look up in my psych book to see if there's a cure. Probably I'm the only one in the universe that has it and there won't be any info on it that I can research. If I was a psycho killer they could probably do something but I just bet there's nothing about people sitting in mirrors and scaring innocent bystanders like *moi.*

Somehow, I got through the day and the last bell rang and I was emancipated from Grover Cleveland H.S. Jimmy had Chess Club so I had to walk. I don't mind. Kathi Mueller lives in my direction and we always walk together. I just thought of something— it seems half of my friends' names end in "I"—there's Missi and Kathi and Teri and Joni and somebody else, I can't think of her name right now but it'll come to me. I wonder if they're all the same ethnic group or what! Patti. That's the one I couldn't think of. Most of them dot the "i" in their names with these little hearts. That's incredibly brilliant, isn't it?

The second Kathi turned down her street and we yelled goodbye to each other, I began to think about that darned mirror person again. I tried to think about other things, like a report I had to do for soch on the Kallikacks, this retarded family in New Jersey who all ate paint chips or something, but my mind kept returning to the face I'd seen in the mirror. The Kallikacks, I think was their name, was this famous family in sociology who lived in New Jersey somewhere in the hills and intermarried and did nasty things like that and ended up mentally challenged. Actually, more like mentally triple-dared. I think my former boyfriend, Chris, was a distant cousin. Just kidding—his last name was Chroninger, which is English, I believe, whereas Kallikacks is Russian or something. Still...

It was a big report, worth one third of my semester grade and I hadn't even started on it, but all I could think of was what I'd seen in the mirror that morning.

When I got home, no one was there. Dad was at work and Mom was probably down at the grocery unloading her coupons. And Mike? Probably playing with his little criminal friends. Usually, I would be ecstatic if Mike wasn't there, as he feels his mission in life is to totally drive me bazonkas, but this time I would have almost welcomed his presence. I studiously avoided the hall mirror when I came in and kept my eyes averted from the one in the living room.

I kind of messed around at first, looking at Mom's magazines, taking off my old nail polish, eating about two dozen chocolate chip cookies and just killing time in general. Finally, my kidneys were about to explode. There was no way around it. I'd have to go into the bathroom.

While I was sitting there, I was aware of the mirror in front of me, but thankfully, it was high enough from where I was that I couldn't see my reflection. This is ridiculous, I remember thinking. Even if there is someone in the mirror they haven't done anything to harm me. All day long, ever since I'd seen Miss Blue Eyes that morning, I'd known what I was going to have to do. The only way to get over this fear was to face it.

And, logically, the downstairs bathroom was the best place to confront whoever or whatever it was, lurking in mirrors. Just in case something did happen,

I'd be found there quicker. No one will come into my room unless it's a national emergency. Once in a while, Mom sneaks in and the way I know she does is at supper she'll diss me, saying she's going to call the exterminators and thanks to me they'll qualify for the bulk rate. I don't think it's that bad myself. Granted, it's a bit messy, but I have my own system and whenever I clean it up to her Better-Homes-and-Gardens specifications, I can never find anything in a hundred years. Who keeps shoes in the closet? It's so dark in there I'd have to hunt up a flashlight every time I needed a pair. I've tried to explain to her that if she doesn't want me to be late to school, let me organize *my* space in my own way, but she makes this funny sound with her nose and cracks on me. I sincerely hope when I get to be her age and have children I give my daughter more latitude than I get. I think she ate too much sugar before they found out it was bad for you and did stuff to your chromosomes or something.

I ran the water in the sink, kind of avoiding the mirror at first. I took a drink, using my hand as a cup. I know it's not ladylike, but if I ran to get a glass every time I needed a drink I'd die of dehydration.

Then I looked. Ohmygod.

There she was all right. Old Miss Blue Eyes. I forced myself to stare at her. At first nothing happened. I stared until I thought my eyeballs were about to bleed. Then, I noticed it. She was smiling at me. I thought maybe I had a grin on my own face but I felt it with my hands and all I felt was a wet frown. Wet because my hands were sweating. Big-time. Worse than a mid-term exam or a first-date sweat. And my heart was beating so fast I thought it'd blow up. There really *was* someone behind the mirror.

Oh lordy.

CHAPTER FOUR

"I know you're in there." I don't know why I said that. Stupido! What else was there to say, though?

"I'm glad you decided to talk to me."

If I hadn't already just gone, I would have wet Calvin on the spot. She spoke. To me. With my own voice, only not out loud. It was more like in my head. It's lucky I wasn't an old-fashioned Southern belle like in Gone with the Wind. I'd have come down with the vapors, sure as my name wasn't Scarlett O'Hara, girlfriend. I came close enough as it was. My knees turned to Cheez-Whiz and I had to grab the sink to stay up. I don't know what I expected her to say. "Take me to your leader," I suppose, or, "We've got you surrounded. Surrender, earthling." I guess I didn't expect her to say *anything* because I didn't really expect there to be a person in the mirror. Now what was I going to do? I had sure enough confronted my fear and here it was, gabbing at me like we were both in the same gym class.

I did the dumb thing.
I spoke to her.

CHAPTER FIVE

"Who are you?"

Original, huh?

"I am you," she answered. What do you think of that? She intoned the words, kind of like Charlton Heston giving out the Ten Commandments in that old movie that's on TV sometimes.

"I don't understand."

"It's simple. I'm you, Elizabeth. You created me."

This was getting bizarre. Getting *bizarre*? That's like saying "this is getting damp" when you're on the crest of a tidal wave.

"Please," I said. "Just tell me who you are and what's going on here. I don't feel very well. This is a dream, right? You're the ravioli I ate last night!"

"I'm sorry, Elizabeth. I don't mean to upset you. Don't be afraid of me. I won't harm you."

I didn't say anything.

"You see, *you* created me. When you were six years old. Don't you remember?"

Boy, did I ever! Like a prison tattoo I'd woke up with.

"The only way I can be created is by someone on your side of the mirror. And I couldn't have been created by just anyone. It requires someone with an overactive imagination."

Lucky me! She sounds just like my mom. Overactive imagination, my behind! My imagination wasn't any more overactive than anyone else's I know. She kept on talking and I listened. I didn't have much choice. She was turning out to be Chatty Cathy with blue orbs.

"You see, our universes are twin worlds. Whatever is reflected in a mirror has an exact duplicate in my world. Some of your scientists and philosophers have guessed at our existence but they always get it wrong. They assume there's some kind of other dimension when we're both really in the same dimension. The only thing is, all *you* can see is a still image. Sort of like looking at a snapshot, except that it moves when you do. More like a movie I guess is how you'd explain it. But we have a restriction you don't."

This ought to be primo, I thought. Sort of the Land of Oz with disclaimers. I wondered again if I was in a dream but the pinch I gave myself felt real enough. I was in your basic state of 3-D terror, but I was also fascinated by what she was telling me.

"We are basically a slave world over here. All we can ever do is exist as your reflection. Unless…"

She stopped here. Just stopped talking. It made

me crazy. Unless what? Was I supposed to guess what the "unless" was? Was this twenty questions? I kept wishing my mother would walk in and see Miss Blue Eyes talking to me so I'd know I wasn't going over the falls, mentally.

"Unless what?" I had to ask, didn't I? Me and my famous big mouth.

"Unless a person imagines there's someone behind the mirror. Like you did when you were six."

"What difference would that make?" I finally found my voice. "I'm sure there are millions of people who imagined what I did. On this block alone, there are probably ten." I was thinking of old Mrs. King who lived three doors down and saw cockroaches crawling all over her about once a month. Usually right after she put out a bushel basket full of Old Granddad empties for the trashman.

"You're right. I'm not the only one in a mirror. There's more of us than you know. But not millions. Maybe a few thousand. It takes more than just imagining there to be someone there for there to be someone there."

That was a brain-twister if I ever heard one. A bunch of gobbledygook if you ask me. I was more confused than ever, but she didn't let me down with the crystal-clear explanations.

"There are some other conditions. For instance, you have to be looking at yourself in a mirror when you imagine there to be another world there, and you have to really, *really* believe there is another world.

"And that doesn't even guarantee you'll see someone other than yourself—create your double, so to speak.

"There are some other things that have to be just right. Like atmospheric pressure, temperature, things like that. We're not even sure about that; we just think those things make a difference. The magnetic field, too."

Now, I wish I'd paid more attention in science class. She was saying there was a whole world back there with her in her mirror world. I was getting more and more spooked. I could feel the goose bumps on my arms and they were roughly the size of tennis balls. She kept on with her dissertation. I felt like I was on the set of Weird Science.

"The biggest component necessary to achieve trans-starence—our term for what happens—is the electrical activity of the particular individual's brain at the time. It seems to be a combination of electrical impulses and chemical activity and just a few of you seem to have the proper combination to bring us to life."

Just what I wanted to hear. I had some kind of mutant brain. Now I'm a mirror freak because the zinc in my brain shorts out differently than anyone else on the planet. Didn't she know teenagers would rather be green than different? Like my dad says, in a snide little voice, "I suppose if all your friends walked off a cliff you'd follow them." You'd better believe I would! I'd be second in line, especially if the leader was Sandra Dean, the most popular girl in the universe. I've seen what happens to people when they look or act different. They sure don't get sixteen offers to the Senior Prom. No thank you! When I get to be a hundred and ten then I'll work on being an individual. Until then I'd like to have a few friends!

"Now—you create us, but once we're here we kind of develop on our own. Within limits. We can't change our appearance too much—we're pretty well stuck with whatever you look like—" well, I swear, "—but I got to change mine 'cause you were wishing you had blue eyes when you first imagined me."

I not only create Mutant Mirror Person, I give her a better eye color than what I'm stuck with. Why couldn't life have been reversed and she gave me blue eyes and kept the pine-cone-colored ones for herself? Sometimes life is just a dog-eat-dog world and you're forever wearing Milk Bone underwear.

"There's a lot more to it, like how you're wondering where I was for all those years when you didn't see me—see, I can read your mind when you're facing me—and I'll explain it all to you eventually, but I thought you might like some good news. You look like you need some."

Yeah, like this is all a dream and I promise never again to eat that many chocolate chip cookies. No such luck. Blue Eyes was really there. I was as wide-awake as Anne Boleyn was two minutes before she lost her head. She was babbling on again.

"Now that you've acknowledged me and we've

communicated, there's something cool we can do, provided we both agree to it."

Great. Now she thinks we're best buds. Next thing, we'll be having jammy parties, freezing each other's bras. I waited, afraid to ask what delightful thing it was we could do. I didn't have to wait long. She was about as anxious to let me in on her secret as five-year-olds are to open their Christmas presents.

"We can trade places."

CHAPTER SIX

Trade places.

Like I'm frothing at the mouth to get inside that mirror! Does she think my I.Q. lost a couple of zeroes?

"Uh, I don't think that's something I'd like to do especially, this current century," I offered.

"Don't be so quick to dismiss the idea," she answered. "Just think about the possibility for a while. Don't you think it would be exciting?"

Yeah, like being shot into space strapped onto the side of a Saturn rocket. The first five nanoseconds would be a thrill, but after that...? I didn't vocalize my thought but she wasn't kidding when she'd said she could read my mind.

"I'm not familiar with a Saturn rocket. Is it fun?"

"You're spooky!" I said, watching my/her eyes grow about as big as my fat Aunt Minnie's dessert plates. (My cousin Sam calls Aunt Minnie Aunt *Maxie* if that helps you get a fix on how big her dessert plates are.) She *was* spooky! "How can you read my mind?"

"It has something to do with the electromagnetic field around you. I can't explain it and it can only happen when you're looking into the mirror into my eyes."

I lowered my eyes, picked out a spot on my chin and thought, that's just about the last time I do that. Or if I do, I'm crossing my eyes or something. A terrible thought struck me.

"How long have you been able to read my mind?"

Her answer was swift. Too swift.

"Since you were six."

"What have you read?"

"Oh, lots of stuff. How's Jimmy?"

She knows everything. My gosh, some of the things I've thought about Jimmy! Some of the things I've thought about anybody! Some of my thoughts were so personal I wouldn't even tell them on an overnight camping trip to my best friend. This was gross, terrible! Then, I realized Miss Blue Eyes wasn't a for-real person. I had created her. I stared back at myself. Maybe I could un-create her.

"No, you can't."

I turned from the mirror and took a step back over to the stool and sat down, head in hands. It was hopeless. What was I going to do? I felt like bawling, but if I did, she'd probably materialize and hand me a tissue. There was no doubt about it—I was a slave to Blue Eyes. Might as well hang a ball and chain around my neck and call in the dogs. This was a disaster. This was a ground-zero nuclear blast. I wasn't ever going to escape her. Ever.

I remembered this book I'd read last year about some black lady, and in it she made the statement that "education gives a person their freedom." Maybe that was the answer. Maybe if I learned everything there was to learn about this mirror person I could make her vanish and get my life at least back up to the bargain basement. It would be a pleasure to only have to worry about getting into college or whether science would ever come up with a cure for acne. Those seemed like very faraway and very childish worries compared with the situation I faced right now. I got back up and stepped over to the mirror and faced it squarely.

"Why would you want to come out here if it's so great in there?"

"That's easy, Liz. It looks like a lot of fun there, too."

I hate it when someone calls me Liz. Here I was, almost seventeen and she wants to give me this little kid's name. She was blathering again.

"See, it's okay in here—for instance, since it would all be new to you, you'd enjoy it. But me, I've never been anywhere but in mirrors all my life and I'd like to see some of your world. You'd get a kick out of what you can do in here, too, believe me."

"I've seen you in more than one mirror. Can you get around to different ones?"

"Sure. There's one little drawback. I can only get around from this side of the mirror. I've seen lots of things, trees, parks, playgrounds, stuff like that, but I can't get out to enjoy those things. Sometimes I've been out with you in your compact and it looks wonderful! Grass and hills and going fast in cars. I love that stuff. But—" I could see a pout in her lower lip and I felt sorry for her in that moment, "—you never have it open for more than a minute or two, and then boom! you slam me shut and I'm back in the dark, wondering where we are and what it looks like. I can go to another mirror any time I want, but lots of times I just want to stay with you and do what you're doing."

"I didn't realize…"

"There's other things too, Elizabeth. You seem to feel things, *physical* things that I've never felt. I've heard you say 'ouch' and I've never had an ouch thing happen to me. Or an 'oh boy!' thing, either. I'm just kinda in here, looking out, not feeling anything. I think I've got the capability—last week you were sad and crying and I sort of felt sad too, I think. When you weren't looking for a second I put my hand up to feel the tears on our face and I couldn't feel them. What are they like? If I had a real body, I think I would experience and feel some of the things people in your world do. I just want a chance to try. If I could have even five minutes of being real, I think it would satisfy me for the rest of my life."

The way she put it almost made me feel guilty.

Like it was my fault or something. I never asked for her to come along. It's not my fault she's a mirror person. Or is it? I couldn't think. Everything was happening so fast.

"Just think, Elizabeth. If you were in here, you could travel to any mirror you wanted and find out all kinds of secrets. Haven't you ever wished you could spy on someone or see something secret?"

Well, who wouldn't? This mirror stuff might not be so bad after all. I decided to try and keep an open mind.

"Yeah. Maybe sometimes I do wonder what it would be like."

"Like Jimmy?"

She could read my mind all right.

"Maybe."

"If you wanted, I could go over to his house right now and see if I can catch him in front of a mirror. I've done it before. I could come back and tell you what he's doing."

It was tempting but I couldn't let her.

"Or better yet, we could trade places and *you* could go look for yourself. Or anywhere else you wanted to go. I can show you how to hide in a mirror so they'll never notice you."

Wow, that was tempting! I almost gave in, but some small, quiet voice inside me kept saying, no, no, no. Actually, it was more like a scream. I was scared to death to even consider climbing into that mirror or whatever you did to get into it.

She was as persistent as a vacuum-cleaner sales-man. I think she sensed the curiosity that was burning inside me.

"I know you're frightened, Elizabeth, but there's no need to be. You can't get hurt in here and we can trade places back and forth easier than boys find dirt. You know, I think we're going to be great friends. I've never had a girlfriend. C'mon, let's trade! You'll love it in here."

Something told me to be cautious but something else told me I'd be nuts to pass up this opportunity. Besides, she didn't seem that bad. Kind of nice, actually.

"How do we do it?"

CHAPTER SEVEN

I never should have asked her that. The crack she had in the doorway just got wider. About wide enough to drive a fleet of semis through.

"It's easy, Elizabeth. You just look into my eyes and say, 'I want to trade places.' That's all there is to it. It's the easiest thing in the world."

Easy, indeed. There had to be more to it. It seemed too simple. And how did I get back out? I didn't have to ask; she was in her mind-reading mode.

"Simple. You just have to look into my eyes again and say the same thing, 'I want to trade places,' and we automatically change places. There's nothing to it. C'mon. What do you say, girlfriend? We'll both have some fun."

It was tempting. All of a sudden, I could think of about a million things I could do from the other side of a mirror. I could spy on all sorts of people. Like Jimmy. My mind was quickly being made up but I still had reservations.

"You sure that's all I have to do?"

"That's it. I give you my word."

"Wait a tish. How do I get around in there once we've traded places?"

"That's a good question, Elizabeth, and it shows you've got your thinking cap on. It's easy. I can't explain it to you, but once you're in here you'll just know how. There's nothing to it. Trust me."

As soon as she said "trust me," I had this queer thought about my little brother, Mike. I bet he's said "trust me" at least a kazillion times and each time I did, I ended up walking around half the day with shoe polish rings around my eyes or something. But I was committed now. Curiosity is my biggest flaw and is always getting me in a jam.

"Okay," I said, deciding. "Can we just do it for a minute and then trade right back? Just so I can see what it feels like?"

She got this big dreamy smile on her face and all of a sudden I knew I could trust her. Poor thing, trapped in there all her life. I could certainly give up a minute or two to let her experience what I took for granted. It was the least I could do.

"Sure. Just look into my eyes and say, 'I want to trade places.' And be sincere."

I'll do it, I thought. Why not? If the first man hadn't stepped out of the space ship onto the moon, little kids all over would still think it was made out of green cheese. What I was about to do was heroic. Scientific, too. I was taking a step for all mankind. I would be some kind of super explorer. Why, someday I could end up in history books and Mr. Bormuth would have to teach kids about me.

I was telling myself all this stuff, when inside I was shaking like Mrs. King during one of her cockroach attacks. I was doing what I always do: talking myself into trouble. Oh well, in for a penny, in for a dollar, as my dad says.

"Let's do it," I said, finally. "But only for a minute."

I closed my eyes tight, took a deep breath and held it. I opened them and focused back on the mirror, staring into our eyes, and said, "I want to trade places."

CHAPTER EIGHT

Nothing happened. I was still staring at her eyes and everything was exactly the same. It hadn't worked. I was still in the bathroom, looking into the mirror. There was the wall with the flowered wallpaper and the towel rack with mom's pink towels. I felt all sorts of emotions, elation at not being in the mirror and sadness that it hadn't worked. Then, I noticed that something was wrong. Miss Blue Eyes wasn't. Blue-eyed, that is. Her eyes had changed color and were like mine. Brown.

Something else was wrong. I couldn't put my finger on it right away, but as I kept staring at her, it came to me. It was dark behind me. I could just barely see that out of the corner of my eye. Slowly, I began turning my head, still keeping my gaze locked with hers, until I had to break contact, and I turned my head completely around, quickly, and then back. I was sure my hair was standing straight out.

There was nothing behind me. Nothing but the

blackest darkness I had ever seen.

I have never been more totally scared in my life than I was at that exact moment. The terror welled up so swiftly my ears rang with the silent scream that jangled from every nerve ending and pore in my body.

I was in the mirror.

CHAPTER NINE

I forced myself to calm down. So I was in the mirror. So what? It didn't feel bad or anything. It felt just the same as before. Before I was an official mirror person. Could I talk, I wondered? I tried out my voice. This teeny quavering mouse squeak came out.

"Am I in the mirror?" I sounded like one of the munchkins in The Wizard of Oz.

"Yes, Elizabeth, and your eyes are blue now. Didn't you always want blue eyes?"

I could think of things I wanted more. Like getting out of this mirror now that I was in it.

"Yeah, that's nice, I guess—who knows? I can't see them. They look brown to me when I look at you. Anyway, this has been some fun, but I'm ready to come out now. *I...want...to...trade—*"

I said it slowly and deliberately and so loud I was sure I was shouting. It didn't work. I was still in the mirror. Then I knew why. She wasn't looking at me. Her eyes were downcast, gazing down at the sink.

"Look at me, Blue Eyes!" I screamed. I didn't know what else to call her. She didn't look up, but kept looking down at the sink. I heard my mother come in the front door and call my name.

"Elizabeth! Where are you, hon?"

"Here I am, Mom. In the mirror. Come and get me. Please!"

Miss Blue Eyes didn't look up, but I saw her smile and it was a different kind of smile now. It was positively evil. She turned her head in the direction of mom's voice and said, "I'm coming, Mom. Be there in a minute." She glanced in the mirror. "She can't hear you, you know. Or see you. Only I can."

Then she was gone. Disappeared. I heard the door to the bathroom slam and I was left staring at my mom's pink towels.

CHAPTER TEN

It's been two forever weeks now and I'm still inside the mirror. I know how to get out. All I have to do is get eye contact with Miss Blue Eyes long enough to say the words. And it's not like she doesn't use mirrors. She's in front of them constantly. She's got this trick she does that keeps me imprisoned here. She looks obliquely into the glass, almost never straight on. Oh, sometimes she'll look directly at me but never long enough for me to say the magic words. I can say it pretty fast, just not fast enough. I guess she's had years to practice what she's doing. She's a real pro.

What a chump I was!

She was right about one thing. It's easy to go from mirror to mirror in here. It wasn't totally black in here like I first thought. There are thousands of tiny little pinpricks of light, kind of like stars. Trillions of them. They're all mirrors. You just kind of "think" where you want to go and you're there.

I've been all over the map. Once I stopped crying, that is.

I went and saw the actor Christian Slater once. Was I surprised! You'd think a big movie star like that would be out partying with a bunch of other movie mavens or at least doing something movie star-ish. I couldn't believe what he was doing when I saw him! He was just sitting there in this easy chair reading a book. Not only that, but the book was one of those thick ones they make you read in English class. *The Brothers Karamazov* by Dostoevsky. He was reading it for *fun*. I guess so, anyway; I mean, the movie studio wouldn't make you read stuff like that, would they? I could have died! Everybody knows he looks so deep all the time, but you know how it is—in the back of your mind you just figure that's the way his manager or whatever wants him to come across for his public, but it's really true. He *is* deep. I wish I could tell my friends, especially Amy Wempel, about this. She thinks he's the ultimate actor already and if she knew he was sitting around reading great classics when nobody was making him, well, she'd probably want to hitchhike over to his house and propose on the spot.

You should see what Liz is doing to my life.

Yesterday, I was in the big mirror in the front room and she waltzed in from school. I won't even tell you what she's doing to my hair these days— only that the world isn't ready for it yet. My mom was sitting on the sofa, sorting through her recipe box and she looked up and said, "Hi, Sweetie. How was school?"

"School's for schmucks. I'm thinking about quitting."

My mom's hand flew to her mouth. "Elizabeth! I can't believe my ears. I—"

She interrupted. "And I told you, I don't want to be called Elizabeth anymore. My name is Liz. Say it, Mother. Liz, Liz, Liz!" She stormed off up to my room, which, incidentally, is totally trashed. A thousand times worse than I ever kept it. I'll never find anything in there again.

As it stands right now, I'm grounded until the age of eighty-two, provided, that is, that I can ever get out of here. I've dropped Jimmy as my boyfriend and now I date about six zillion other guys, most of them about the age of my dad and none I'd be caught dead with if it was really me out there. I've sassed my parents, hit my brother and stolen from my married sister Sienna's purse. I sneak into my parents' bedroom at night and hear them saying things like, "What do you think about boarding school for Elizabeth?"

My life is ruined. It's been thermonucleared. I can't even pick up the pieces; it's all in subatomic particles.

Part of my new life *has* been interesting, I will admit. I've gone lots of places and seen tons of stuff. Christian Slater and stuff like that. It's like Miss Blue Eyes—*Liz*—said, I can go almost anywhere. I can't explain how you do it—if you were in here you'd see how instantly, but what good does it do me? On this side of the mirror you're not real. I don't even feel real. I can't feel my body and I'm never hungry or ever have any bodily functions, which saves on toilet paper but not on my sensitive psyche. I do seem to have all my emotions intact and I remember Liz saying something about how she was lacking in that. It must have something to do with which side of the mirror you come from originally.

There are other people in here too. Oh, boy. I can't tell you how excited I am about *that*. The first time I realized that, I nearly jumped out of my skin. If I actually *had* skin, I would have. I was staring out at an empty living room, silently mourning the loss of my freedom, when this voice right at my elbow, said, "Hey, what's going on, chickie?" in this *conversational* tone of voice, which made it scarier. As soon as I got my heart rate down to a thousand beats per kilosecond, I said, "What's going on is that I just peed my pants, lamebrain, or I would have if I could still pee. Who are you? And who calls people *chickie*? You just land from the nineteen fifties?" It was some Australian guy, a total zero. If he looks like most of the boys in Australia, I think I'll stay Up Over. I haven't seen that many zits on a face since they messed up our last order from the Hut and I overdosed on the pepperoni. You'd think a kid with that many pus factories wouldn't go near a mirror, let alone stare into one long enough to create a twin.

"I'm just being friendly," he said, with this big pout on his kisser, and then he vanished, gone away somewhere in mirrorland. Probably to hang out with some other Clearasil junkies. Good riddance.

Since then, I see people all over the place in here. There have been times, like at Nancy Gold's birthday party when I felt I was suffocating with all of the people around me. A bunch of zombies. We don't talk much or anything. Like I would want to! Talk isn't the right word anyway—there's a kind of communication between us, sort of like mind-reading that sounds like a voice, but they're weird folks, even worse than Liz, and I have nothing in common with them, I'm sure! That time, at Nancy's party, with all those ghouls around me, I kept thinking of that old TV ad for "Mr. Microphone." You know, where these losers are all standing around, looking at their shoes, until Mr. Party Animal gets out his Mr. Microphone and then, boy, hey! do they ever start rocking! They all break out in a rousing chorus of "Michael, Row The Boat Ashore" or something stupendously cool like that. These people were even creepier than the TV people—I don't think they'd come alive at *anything*, much less a banana-yellow battery-operated plastic mike from FAO Schwartz's Under Six Department.

There's this one girl, isn't too bad. Her name is Betty and she's about my age. The sad thing is, she's been my age for about a hundred and sixty years. The Betty who created her died of the plague or something when she was seventeen, back in the eighteen hundreds, and guess what? Whatever age your creating human dies at is the age you get to stay forever. Nobody dies in here, but jeezum, what fun it must be to look forward to crawling around the world's mirrors for the next millennium or so! Poor Betty. She was from Indiana, too, which is why she said she stays in the area, but if I'd been here as long as she has, I think I'd relocate. Check out some new scenery or something.

"Betty," I said to her one day. "Did you know Liz?"

At first, she didn't want to answer me, but I kept after her and she admitted she did. "I didn't like her much," she said. She was always saying my eyes were ugly. She was mean."

Betty's eyes were the same color as mine.

She liked to go watch people do things in the mirror. Things they did when they thought they were alone. You know, things with their noses, for example. Yuck! Include me out, I told her, on that one.

I did kind of like her, even if all she wanted to talk about was the good old days when they had what she called "really fun quilting parties," but she'd disappear for days at a time and when she came back and I asked her where she'd been, she'd say she liked to go back to where she'd lived as a girl, some farm just outside of Fairmont, Indiana. The only problem was, the old homestead had been torn down and was now a Dairy Freeze, but she said it wasn't too bad there. It was the hot spot in the town and she knew practically everybody. Fairmont is the town where James Dean, the old-time actor my mom gets goofy-eyed over, is from. Our family was even trucked down there once a couple of years ago by Mom to walk around his grave. Some fun! Most of the other people there weren't much older than me. I don't know why he was such a big deal to someone who wasn't even alive when he was. The kind of person that's maxed out on the shopping scene, I guess, has to manufacture some excitement. Personally, I'd rather spend my time researching how Cheez Whiz is made. I guess the Dean guy got struck down in his prime, according to Mom, and would have been bigger than Tom Cruise if he'd lived, but people say things like that all the time about movie stars when they die young. Like Elvis. My dad is a stitch about Elvis. At Christmastime, we ride around all over town to see the different ways people decorate their yards and stuff, and whenever Dad sees an especially gaudy one, like all twenty-nine members of the Holy Family all lit up in Technicolor plastic, along with all the major Disney animals blinking and nodding, he always says, "Well, Elvis is dead...but his *spirit* lives on." Cracks me up. We've got this neighbor who does his entire house *and* yard in pulsating red lights, along with his tree, which is in front of the living room picture window—*all in red*—and all night long it just throbs and throbs. Especially that blood-red Christmas tree. We call it "The Edgar Allen Poe Memorial House" or, as Dad says, "Subtitled, 'The Tell-Tale Heart.'" If I lived in that house I'd have nightmares until Easter.

Anyway, Betty said to watch what Liz does to my boyfriend and she hit the nail on the head with the hammer with that advice.

Poor Jimmy. He doesn't know what hit him. One day he's got this warm, caring girlfriend (me), and the next day she's telling everyone in the universe all of his deepest secrets (Liz).

"French can't french."

I had just popped over to the girls' bathroom at school at noon to check out the situation. I couldn't believe my ears. Liz was at the center of a bunch of my friends. Girls were coming in for just a second and staying. The crowd kept growing, all of them listening to what they thought were *my* words.

"Worse kisser I ever sucked face with," Liz was going on. "I don't know why she's, er, *I've* kept him for a boyfriend this long." She was talking about my baby, Jimmy French.

It's just plain *odd* in here. I can travel around pretty good around in mirrorland, but I don't always know where Liz is going to be. I'm trying to watch her as closely as I can so I don't miss my chance to escape. I'm sure there have been plenty of times when she was miles away from where I expected her to be and gazing right into a mirror and laughing.

She doesn't go to the same hangouts I always did; she's found her own places to go to and her own crowd to hang around with, and in my opinion her new crowd has sniffed way too much glue. They're hoodlums and jerks and showoffs.

And the way she dresses! Like Tori Spelling used to when she was twelve and as if she'd had to shop on a very skinny budget. In Indiana! If I ever get out of here I'll never be able to go anywhere and hold my head up again. I'll just be lucky to keep from going to prison.

I've found her flaw. It's vanity. She can't pass a mirror without looking at herself. I just have to find a way to exploit that.

CHAPTER ELEVEN

Two weeks ago, after she'd tricked me into the mirror, I waited for almost an hour, hoping she'd return and laugh, saying she was just joking. Yeah, right. I finally realized she'd planned this all along and wasn't ever going to let me out. I guess I shouldn't plan on being a card sharp, what with the quick way I size people up.

I went looking for her. It was easy. First stop was the hall mirror, and sure enough, there she was. Telling my mother not to wait up for her; she didn't know when she'd be home that night. Turns out, she didn't come back home until the next morning.

I was furious. I would never have dared tell Mom something like that. Our family has always had this big deal about being polite to one another and using common courtesy, and it hurt to see the look on Mom's face when she asked where she was going and Liz said, "None of your business. I'm not a baby." Mom thought that person was me! I yelled and screamed at her from inside the mirror, but of course she couldn't hear or see me. It just killed me when I saw the tears in her eyes and the look on her face when Liz slammed the door shut behind her.

After Mom went into her bedroom to begin her nervous breakdown, I resisted the temptation to follow her. It just didn't seem right. Instead, I went to Jimmy's house, and there he was, lying on his bed, listening to his CD player. I just stood there and watched him from his bedroom mirror, tears running down my cheeks, because I couldn't talk to him or touch him and probably never would again.

It wasn't ten minutes later that *she* appeared, barging right into his bedroom without even knocking. She went right over to him and jumped on top of him where he was laying. He didn't see or hear her since he had his back to the door and his earphones on, but when she jumped on him he threw the earphones off and gave her a big hug. That hurt!

She whispered something to him. I couldn't hear what it was, but Jimmy got this serious look on his face and said, "Elizabeth, we agreed to wait. I love you, hon. This just isn't the right time. Besides, my mother is right downstairs."

She stood up, put her hands on her hips and said in this icy voice, "I should have known you'd say something like that, Jimbo. That's okay, buster, I'd rather have a *real* man anyway. See ya around, lame-o." She flounced out the door and there Jimmy was with the same look on his face that I'd just seen on Mom's. I couldn't stand to see him like that, so I cut out, thinking I'd try to find Liz, see what part of my life she was going to trash next.

I didn't have a clue where to look. I must have searched dozens of mirrors, all over town. Brand X, the record store, all the shops in the mall I thought she might go to; I even went to the truckstop at the edge of town and looked out of all their mirrors except the ones in the men's bathroom. No Liz. Anywhere. She had vanished off the face of the earth. I searched for hours and then it got late and places started closing. Once they turned their lights off, I could see very little.

I discovered a funny thing. When you're a mirror person, you don't need sleep. In fact, you *can't* sleep. To keep from going Space City, you have to find mirrors in places that don't close and in our town that wasn't easy. I ended up going to a tavern I never before had even wanted to walk by, just because it was the only place still open, except for an all-night gas station.

That's where I found her.

CHAPTER TWELVE

She was sitting at the bar and she had a real drink in front of her! If I had had a real body I would have fallen down. She was talking and flirting with some guy who I couldn't make out real well since I was in the mirror behind the bar and it hadn't been cleaned in about thirty years, and there were whiskey bottles in front of me. I could see parts of her face, depending on how she moved, but I never got a clear look at the guy, only that he looked about as old as the oldest living ex-president, that guy from Georgia, and uglier than a pop quiz. Mom will kill me, I thought. Not to mention what's happening to my reputation which Charles Manson wouldn't even take now. If I get out of here, I'll have to pack a bag and leave home. I couldn't take watching her anymore. I cut out and went to the only other all-night place, Joe's Gas, and stayed there all night. I know the kid who works there nights, Joe's kid, Joe Junior. His claim to fame is that he broke his leg blocking on the play in which Jerry Lerendet ran ninety-six yards before being tackled on the one-yard line, the biggest play in our school's history. We lost the game but no one cared much, mostly because of that fantastic run. Personally, I didn't get it—I mean, we lost the game. But no one seemed to think that was important because of that long run.

Anyway, that's all that Junior ever talked about. He would find a way to bring it up in practically every conversation he ever had. Somebody would be talking about the weather or the war in Afghanistan and here Junior butts in with something like, "Yeah, it was raining like this the night I broke my leg in two places when Jerry Lerendet ran ninety-six yards," or, "You talk about a war! It was a war the night I threw that block that sprung Lerendet for his run." Stuff like that. You get the picture. It got a mention in Sports Illustrated, in the section way in the back where you have to have a relative point it out and use a magnifying glass to read it, and Junior bought up about three hundred copies of the issue and had that page framed and everything. There's a framed copy on the wall behind the cash register at the gas station and I'll bet anything he's got his bedroom walls papered with it. People used to say, give it a rest, Junior, but he never caught on and after a while they just let him talk. Other than that, he was a decent enough kid, even though I'm pretty sure he was in the bunch that teepeed Mary Lou Zanzibar's house and her dad saw them throwing the toilet paper and ran out to yell at them and tripped over a rake her little brother had left in the yard and suffered this mild concussion and spent the night in the hospital, but then it was never proven for sure that Junior was with whoever it was, and I think you ought to give people the benefit of the doubt. Anyway, even if he was in that group, they certainly didn't start out to give Mr. Zanzibar a concussion. They only teepeed their house because Mary Lou was popular and I think Junior had a crush on her. In a way, it was kind of Mr. Zanzibar's own fault; if he had just stayed in the house it would never have happened, and his own son had left the rake where it shouldn't have been in the first place. Sometimes people don't bother to figure out all the extenuating circumstances and then put the blame where it doesn't belong. It's an adult trait, one I hope I never get.

Anyway, Mr. Zanzibar was positive he'd seen Junior along with six other boys, and for a long time he wouldn't buy gas at Joe Senior's gas station. But it all seems to have blown over now, because that very first night I stayed there in the mirror behind the cash register, who comes in but Mr. Z himself and Junior even calls him by his first name, which is Herbert. If I was Mr. Zanzibar and was stuck with that, I would never let anybody call me anything but "Mr. Z," not even my own wife and children.

I could hear them talking just as clear as cellophane since I'm like two feet away, and I nearly collapsed when Herbert told Junior he'd just gone by Grossman's Tap where he saw Elizabeth Downing sitting at the bar, and she wasn't drinking ginger ale, and she wasn't talking to her science lab partner. He told Junior he was thinking about notifying Elizabeth's parents and Junior said, so help me Hannah, "Well, Herbert, this is like when I broke my leg in two places blocking on Jerry Lerendet's run. I didn't want my parents to know but somebody told them, and in the long run I was glad to see them at the hospital. You can imagine the pain I was feeling." I couldn't believe this guy. His parents were sitting on the fifty-yard line when it happened. He went on, "I think, in the long run, Elizabeth will thank you, too."

No, you idiot, I screamed, but of course neither of these two rocket scientists could hear a syllable, and then Mr. Z is gone to do his duty and Junior is breaking his neck to get the news out to all points about Elizabeth Downing.

At the rate she was going, Liz was going to have me in slam doing heavy time in about a week.

An idea began to form.

First, I'd gain her confidence, make her think I no longer wanted to be out of here, that this was the E Ticket to Disneyworld as far as I was concerned.

That was the first step.

CHAPTER THIRTEEN

She was in the bathroom fixing her hair the next day. If you could call it that. Personally, I'd call it "un-fixed." I forced a smile and appeared.

"Hi, Blue Eyes. I've got an idea."

She ducked down out of sight. Slowly, she inched back into view, careful to stare at her/my chin and not meet my/her eyes.

"Don't call me Blue Eyes. My name is Liz."

What nerve! I decided to swallow my anger and not let it show. Anyway, I hated the nickname "Liz." She could have it.

"Okay, Liz. Liz, I've been thinking."

She hooted, sounded like one of those owls on "Wild Kingdom."

"What have you got to think about? You're nothing but a mirror person. And you're going to be one forever. How do you like that?"

About as much as I like a pound of pure cane sugar on a cavity, thanks.

"Actually, Liz, I do sort of like it in here. I can go anywhere I want, and best of all, I don't have to do homework."

"Yeah," she said. "Homework *is* a bummer. I've decided not to do any."

I'd noticed that. "Smart thinking, Liz. What waitress needs algebra down at the ol' truckstop? I'll bet you can figure most of your tips with just basic third-grade math."

I saw her furrow her brow and knew she was trying to figure out if I was dissing her or what. I went on, quickly.

"Yeah, you know, the longer I'm in here, the more I like it. In fact—" I paused for dramatic effect just the way Mr. Dawes had taught us in drama class, "—even if you wanted to, I'd refuse to come out now."

I knew this was too much for her to swallow and I was right. She gave a snort that would have sexually aroused a stallion. No matter. Before I was done with her she was going to be convinced I loved it in here.

"It's great in here," I went on, "but there is something I miss. Like riding on the roller coaster at Indiana Beach. I'd love to go for a ride on that again."

She looked at my eyes for just the tiniest second before she glanced away. I'd never noticed how mean her eyes were. They were filled with cruelty. I had created this? I felt nauseous, like the first time I saw hair under my armpits.

"Well, you can just eat your heart out, 'cause that's something you're never going to do again." She hesitated and then spoke again, a conciliatory note creeping into her voice. "Is it fun?"

"Is it! It's the best! A super rush!"

She didn't answer, only flounced away, out of the bathroom and my sight. I felt like smashing the mirror with my fists, which was impossible and supremely frustrating.

The rest of that day and all of the evening I followed her around, from mirror to mirror, but she refused to talk whenever I said hi or tried to start a conversation. That night, I spent a bor-ring eight hours at Joe's Gas watching Junior count out change and talk about his big football block. I found myself wishing I could re-break his leg so he'd really have something to talk about. I was almost ready to spend the night anywhere but there, but most places in town, except for a couple of sleazy bars, were dark and closed. I suppose I could have gone to a bigger town or even another country but mirror travel at night was harder and didn't seem worth the effort. And I was sure getting tired of hanging out in bathrooms.

What went on isn't worth repeating. I found out who I wouldn't ever go out with. About eight of Junior's friends showed up and spent hours swilling beer and telling jokes, mostly the kind that put girls down. At least three guys I'd had on my "maybe I'd go out with" list got x'd off and transferred to the not-until-a-talking-geranium-is-elected-president list.

Next morning, I was back at my house, waiting for Liz in the bathroom mirror. It was a Saturday, so I wasn't sure when she'd get up. She was lazy, on top of all her other sterling qualities. This Saturday, she was up early for her, ten o'clock.

I tried talking to her as she put on *my* lipstick. I made my voice sweet, even though I felt like a Sour Tart inside.

"Good morning, Liz."

She just grunted. The best part of her vocabulary.

"Have you given any thought to what we talked about yesterday?"

Again, a grunt. It was like talking to a 4-H pig. The one who *lost* the blue ribbon.

"About the roller coaster, Liz. See, you could go and just open your compact while you were riding and I'd get to ride too."

Silence. Blusher being slapped on. Too thickly. My blusher, bought out of my meager allowance money.

Abruptly, she snapped the compact closed, tossed it in my makeup bag and stalked out of the bathroom.

Great. So far my scheme was working about as well as General Custer's Big Victory Battle Plan.

I zoomed into the front-hall mirror. She was there talking to Mom. I just caught a few words before she turned and walked out of the front door: "...for me. I'm going to Indiana Beach."

My heart flipped a UCLA-cheerleader-class cartwheel and I mentally crossed my fingers. Maybe my plan would work after all!

She left in *her* car. Bought with the money *I'd* been saving for college. I don't even want to think about *that* episode. She bought it the very next day after she trapped me in here. There went my future, speeding away at ten miles to the gallon. Not only did she use my hard-earned bucks, she totally alienated Mom and Dad. There had been a fight that Don King would have loved to promote.

With college in the dumper, I could see my dismal future looming before me. I'm behind this counter, my finger on a cash register key that looks like a hamburger with a Smiley Face. I'm sixty-five years old and wearing a name tag on my uniform. Jimmy walks in with his drop-dead gorgeous wife who's a stock broker and their four lovely kids who have all been accelerated at least six grades in school. I've got this hairnet on to keep my frizzy gray hairs from dropping down on the NastyBurgers and my spine is crooked because of eating too much cat food and not enough milk. Jimmy sees me and goes all white and slips me a five-dollar tip. I thank him for it, prostrating myself on my knees and kissing the hem of his Armani pants. After my twelve-hour shift is over, I feel so terrible I go out right away and buy a cheap gallon of port wine and take it back to the dumpster I live in, pulling a hunk of cardboard over the opening to keep the snow out.

All the while we're driving to Indiana Beach, I'm thinking stuff like this and my feelings for my mirror twin are intense, to say the least. I rode in the rear-view mirror and if you don't think that doesn't make your stomach roll after a couple of miles, watching everything go by backwards! This plan better work!

What I'm hoping for is this. When Miss Blue Eyes gets on the Hoosier Hurricane, she's going to get an experience she's not quite ready for. What I'm counting on is that she'll get so scared when they make that first zooming dive to the ground that she's going to turn to the only friend she's got, me, and that's when I've got her. She'll agree to anything to escape the terror.

At least that's the way I see it in my imagination.

It turns out a little different than I figured.

CHAPTER FOURTEEN

She climbs into the roller coaster seat and doesn't even bother to fasten the seat belt. The attendant finally makes her, but she'd rather ride without it, she says. He makes her though, and already I have a sinking feeling. There was a chance she might have gotten thrown from the car, but thanks to the dimwit attendant, fat chance now.

We start out and she does the strangest thing. She takes her compact, the one that used to belong to me, and opens it and points it dead ahead. She's chosen the seat I always call the "death seat," the very first one, the one I'd have to be flatlining on my CAT scan to even consider putting my body unit into. My only view is *dead* ahead, pun intended. I have a choice—I can stay in the mirror or I can go someplace else. It isn't much of a choice. If I leave, there goes the only opportunity I'll have. If I stay, there's no guarantee she'll turn the mirror around so I can face her.

I stay.

We reach the top of the first drop-off, up where the air is thin and clouds gather. I look around for some angels but they all must be on their coffee break, or maybe it's just too high up for them. We hang up there for two or three lifetimes and I can't tell which would be better, to hang there some more or get it over with. Either option stinks. Then we start falling, barely moving at first and then we're moving at about the speed of light, and I'm aware of three distinct sounds—the whoosh of the roller coaster, a high-pitched keening that seems to be coming from me, and an insane, maniacal laugher that is emanating from Guess Who.

That's right—she loves it. Isn't the least bit frightened. Me? I need a heart pro, the best Mayo Clinic has got. I go through about twenty-nine blackouts and fainting spells, and if I'd had a lunch to lose you could have looked forever with a crew of four thousand and never found it, even with search dogs and metal detectors, I would have lost it so well. All I got was the feeling without the relief. I would have loved to have tossed my cookies all over You-Know-Who.

She ended up riding it again. And again. She rode the darn thing sixteen times, setting what I think is the state record. So much for Plan A.

I didn't have a Plan B.

Unless…

CHAPTER FIFTEEN

Gravity Hill.

That was it!

It just might work.

I was sure I was on the right track. About scaring her, I mean. If I could only figure out a way to scare her enough to make her think I was the only one who could help her, I might convince her to trade places back with me. Or better yet, I could coerce her into doing so. I liked the idea of force more.

Gravity Hill was an optical illusion. It was a spot on a country road about six miles outside of town, near the old abandoned airstrip that crop dusters used years ago, a short stretch of road that appeared to run uphill. If you parked there and put your car in neutral and waited, in a few seconds the car would begin to roll. Uphill! The first time I went there it was the spookiest thing I'd ever experienced. I just about put a puddle on the seat of Jimmy's car. My nice, sweet boyfriend Jimmy set the whole thing up, telling me that aliens landed nearby sometimes and if they were on the prowl in the area they could make your car go uphill with the motor off. His story was that once the car began to roll the aliens were in control of you and you would roll faster and faster until you were highballing it up the hill and then you would shoot up into the heavens to where their spaceship was waiting.

I snickered when he first started talking about it, positive he was pulling my chain, but then he drove me out there at night and it was the spookiest place you ever saw. Nothing around for miles and miles, no houses, people, dogs, cats, or even other cars. Acres and acres of woods on either side before you got there—it looked like something out of the movie *Friday the 13th (Part 1-26)*. When we got there, he turned the jams on the radio off and there was just the sound of the car as it glided along the narrow blacktop, tires hissing in a mist that was more like a heavy dew than a rain, and Jimmy kept talking about aliens and creatures from outer space and going on and on about it so much that by the time we got there (he drove the last hundred yards at about a foot an hour, creeping along), I was half-believing him. Then, we were there and he stopped the car, and when it had come to a complete stop, he turned the engine off and for a long moment there was only the sound of our breathing and some weird night birds, owls or something, hooting or howling or whatever they do, and then, Jumpin' Jimminy, if the car didn't start to move. All...by... itself. *Up*hill.

I died. I mean, I *died.* Went to heaven and the whole bit, screaming all the way. I was screeching and swinging my arms to keep the aliens off of me, and yelling for my mom and dad and the National Guard, and Jimmy and Superman and whoever else I thought might be able to save me, and all the while I didn't even know I was doing it, but I was punching Jimmy on the arm so hard he had bruises for a month, and screaming at him to stop the car and let me out, and I loved Earth and didn't want to leave it, and all kinds of incredibly dumb stuff like that. It was horrible. I mean, it was absolutely the worst experience I had ever been through. I really believed aliens were controlling us and getting ready to suck us into their spacecraft. I had the most fantastic thoughts whirling through my brain all the while, like aliens would force me to marry one of them, one of these little purple and orange dudes and we'd have these rainbow-colored offspring with six arms and feelers and a nose that looks like those little bugles you get on New Year's. It was dark and misting and I swore I could see a glow in the sky up ahead, and I could feel it growing icy-cold, but I realized later it was just because of the perspiration running down my neck. I tell you, I was *not* looking forward to being captured!

It finally crept through my tortured brain that

Jimmy wasn't crying like me but laughing, and that's when I went totally Fruit Loops. For about five minutes, not only was our relationship in peril, but his survival as a human being in his present form was in serious jeopardy. I finally calmed down somewhat and forgave him. About six months later.

Yeah, I thought. Gravity Hill was the ticket. If I couldn't scare the snot out of Miss Blue Eyes there, I'd never be able to.

CHAPTER SIXTEEN

Riding back from Indiana Beach, I broached the idea to her.

"That was fun, wasn't it?" What a liar I'd become!

"It was okay."

You loved it, you witch.

"Anyway, thanks for letting me go along. You get a whole different perspective in a compact, especially when you don't have anything to hold on to. That was the most fun I've had in days." Yeah, the only thing that could compare would be if someone pulled my fingernails out by the roots and then poured turpentine on my fingertips.

"I know something else that's fun, Liz."

She didn't say anything. I didn't either. I was getting to know her personality, if you could call it that. I was willing to bet a hundred bucks that her curiosity was aroused and before long, she'd break down and ask me what it was. Sure enough, ten minutes later she peeked into the rear-view mirror and said,

"What kind of dumb thing would *you* call fun?"

I sniffed. "Well, *you* might not think so, but it's the neatest thing in the world." I shut up. The seed was planted.

"What is it?"

"It's this place I know about, that's all." (I have to inject here that the whole while this exchange was taking place, she was driving at about a hundred and ten miles an hour and all I could see was a blur flashing by…*backwards.* I don't know which was worse, this or the Hoosier Hurricane. It took all my effort to appear calm.)

"So what does that mean—'it's this place I know about'—doesn't sound like anything to me." (She was driving with one hand! Actually, with two fingers!) I wondered what would happen if she got into a wreck and got killed. Would I get killed, too? No. I suddenly remembered Betty. One hundred and sixty year-old-Betty.

"Well, it is. It's a place where UFOs land sometimes. Sometimes you see aliens. You know, beings from outer space. From Mars and Jupiter and places like that. It's the coolest thing. They're weird. It's kind of dangerous, though. I've heard of them capturing earthlings sometimes, and they carry them off to Orbitron 13 or wherever they're from and make love slaves out of them and stuff like that. Experiments. I've heard of experiments they do, like cutting off your arms and sewing them back on so they're growing out of your butt. They don't even use Novocain."

She gave that horsy snort again. I guess it was supposed to be her laugh. A laugh like that makes you want to reward it with a sugar cube or an apple.

"Aliens! And sometimes they carry you off? To be love slaves? How do you even know what a love slave is? You're so lame!

"You know, it might be interesting, after all. It might be worth a yuk or two. Tell me how to get there."

Huh-uh. No way. If I told her how to get there, she might sneak out and go on her own or cover the mirrors so I couldn't be there. I wasn't about to let her trick me.

"I have to take you. I don't know the names of all the roads. I can show you easy enough, though."

"Nah, forget it. Doesn't sound like much to me."

Rats! I'd almost had her. Now I'd have to figure out something else, Plan C, whatever that was. I considered various possibilities, each dumber than the last. I felt like bawling. And then she said, "All right. We'll go."

"We can't go until tonight. The aliens never appear when it's light out. Sunlight gives their skin a rash. And they don't always appear. Just once in a while. And I don't know for sure if they always carry people off. I've just heard rumors...but what I heard was that if they're going to capture you they take your car and everything. You know you're in deep doo-doo if your car starts rolling up the hill and then they just whoosh you up into their spacecraft. There's only one way to stop them at that point."

"What's that?"

I had her! Hey, yoohoo—Miss Potato-Head—don't bring a muskmelon with a nose on it to a battle of wits.

"You have to yell out a word. Nobody knows why, but this word terrifies them and whenever they hear it they drop everything and split for their ship and get out of Dodge. Fast."

"What's the word?"

"You'll laugh."

"No, I won't. What is it?"

"*Louie.* Only it doesn't work if you just say, 'Louie.' You have to say it twice, like this—Louie, Louie—then they're history."

She laughed. I knew she would. She had the manners of a gerbil. But she at least halfway believed me. I could tell she was hooked and that we were going to end up at Gravity Hill. And when the car started rolling and she began yelling, "Louie, Louie," that's when I'd have her. That car was going to continue to roll uphill and nobody in the world would be able to help her cold sweats then. Except me, who would offer to save her if she would just look in the mirror. And guess what would happen then? You guessed it. That would be the end of Miss Blue Eyes. All that would be left to do then would be to convince my parents, Jimmy and about a hundred of my friends that I'd gone temporarily insane and try to patch my life back together.

"Okay," she said after she quit choking on her own laughter. "We'll give it a shot. Tonight, we go to this alien place."

"At nine o'clock. I'll meet you in the front hall mirror."

She hooted again. Hoot all you want, I thought. In just a little while you'll be back in here.

It was four-thirty. Just four and a half hours to go until I'd be free. I couldn't wait.

CHAPTER SEVENTEEN

With four and a half hours to go, I had to do something to kill time. Just hanging around would have driven me insane. I decided to go over to Jimmy's. I was in the hall mirror at home.

But before I could mirror-port—that's what I'd started calling going from mirror to mirror—something happened. Something that took about a thousand years off my life.

Jimmy appeared beside me. In the mirror where I was. Standing beside me, two and a half inches away.

All my internal body organs went into Turbo Freak Alert Meltdown.

"Hi," he said. That's all, just "hi." I can't properly explain what was happening to my heart. It wasn't in its natural rhythm, I can say that much.

"I guess it's a shock to see me, isn't it?"

Shock? No—discovering Ed McMahon on your front porch with a camera crew when you come home from school would be an example of a "shock." This was pretty much way beyond that.

"You think I'm your boyfriend Jimmy, don't you?"

No, actually I think you're John Lennon and I'm Yoko Ono. Won't my parents be pleased we're back.

"I'm not. I'm Liz's boyfriend, Jim. Pleased t'meetcha."

This was fruit. *He* was fruit. *I* was fruit. The entire *universe* was fruit. All of a sudden, I knew where I was. In the psycho ward. Now it all made sense. I could be content here, I decided, putting on my happy face. I can learn to love macramé and I'll bet we have a great croquet course on the yards. I just hope the nurses aren't mean.

"Let me explain."

Oh, please. It would be ever so nice. Please, please, please!

"Liz created me. Sort of like when you created her. I'm a second-generation mirror person. Which means I have restrictions. Like never being able to leave Mirror World.

"But that's okay. I like it here.

"Not like ol' Liz.

"She always wanted to see what it was like out there.

"But she doesn't belong out there.

"She belongs in here.

"With me.

"I guess we both have a problem."

I just listened. The rubber in my legs was beginning to solidify. He was sure one talkative cowboy!

And he had blue eyes. Jimmy's—the *real* Jimmy's—eyes were brown, like my own. Our kids didn't stand a chance. Doomed to eyes of prose, not poetry. The guy, whoever he was, kept talking.

"I can help you solve your problem.

"Which will solve mine."

He talked in paragraphs. I'd never heard that done before. Kind of like this girl Felicia Kearns in my drama class when she was learning her lines. She talked like that. Say a sentence, stop, like it was the end, and then say another one.

I found my voice.

"How?"

"I can show you how to get her back in here."

"You can?" I couldn't hide the thrill this news brought. I grabbed his arm. Nothing there. I'd forgotten we were mirror people.

"Yes, I can. It won't be easy though. You'll have to trick her."

Whoa! Easy with the surprises, big guy.

"I *know* that, Austin Powers. I've already got a plan."

"It won't work." He gave me this little knowing grin. I detest smugness in mirror people. It's obnoxious. And how did he know my plan wouldn't work? How'd he know my plan? Oh no…I knew why. He could read my mind too. This was terrific. Was nothing private in here?

"Not much."

I groaned. Why didn't I have a mind like our

neighbor Mrs. King? Nothing in there but alcohol and cockroaches. Bet the mind-readers in here would give her a wide berth.

"I don't know who Mrs. King is," he was saying, "but if it makes you feel better, I can't read your mind all the time. Only when we're in the same mirror."

I guess that means he'd been in a mirror with me before. Behind me or something. Good thing I hadn't known. I'd be in intensive care, hooked to a monitor and eating my ribeye through a tube.

"All that's unimportant, Elizabeth. What's important is getting Liz back in here and you back in your own world."

Now he was saying something. As a summit meeting, that was a wrap. We were both in complete agreement on the main point of the agenda. I didn't agree with his opinion of my plan, though. I didn't have to voice my feelings. He already knew.

"Go ahead and try it. It won't work. Liz can't be scared and she already suspects a trick. She's pretty smart."

Well, maybe it wouldn't work, but so far he hadn't shown me a better idea. Then he did.

He was right. Next to his scheme, my plan was crappola. But, I'm stubborn and didn't want to give up on my idea. If it didn't work, I'd give his a shot. Besides, I didn't know whether I could trust him. Look what happened the last time I put any faith in a mirror person!

He said something then that made complete sense.

CHAPTER EIGHTEEN

"Even if you get her back in here, you've still got a major problem. How are you going to keep her here? The rest of your life will have to be spent on guard against a slip. Look into her eyes one second too long and she'll trade back with you. Now that she's been out, she can say the phrase and presto! you're back in here and she's out there being a lovable brat."

Lovable brat? Her and baby Hitler. When Attila the Hun ran a day-care center she'd be a lovable brat.

"There's a way to prevent that, though. Keep her in here forever. With me. I love her."

He told me what to do once I was out. To keep her in here permanently. It was brilliant, yet so simple I was surprised I hadn't thought of it myself.

Just then I heard her voice. Jim and I were still in the hall mirror. I could see the back of her head in the kitchen door.

"I'm going out, Ma. Be back later. Maybe."

I could see the living room clock. Eight fifty-five.

And Jim had disappeared.

Liz walked up to the mirror and looked at me.

"Ready?"

I started to say the words but she'd already looked away.

CHAPTER NINETEEN

The whole way there I tried to build the tension. I chattered on and on about aliens and how they hauled unsuspecting earthlings up into their spacecraft. None of it seemed to work, unless you count nonstop giggling as a sign of fear. The truth was, even though I was the only one in the car aware there weren't really any aliens, I was also the only one growing more and more nervous about the possibility as we got nearer to Gravity Hill.

I hate that. It's so fruit. I've been like that all my life. I can know, I mean really *know* something is made up, and I'll still get scared when someone starts talking about it. Like I knew for a fact that Old Man Fishbottom who lives on our corner is not a crazed killer who preys on young girls and chops them up and puts them in his meat loaf, but whenever we have a pajama party and my friends start talking about Mr. Fishbottom, I get the heebie-jeebies and sleep all night with my head under my pillow. And then the next day, when I have to walk by his house, I cross the street to the other side, even though it's out of my way. It's just fruit, that's exactly what it is. Fruit.

That's the current saying at our school. Fruit. It doesn't mean anything and it means everything. It means whatever you want it to mean. Like if something is rude or crude, then it's fruit. If you do something dumb, that's fruit. If a teacher chews you out in front of your classmates, that's fruit. If he chews out your worst enemy, that's *sweet* fruit. You get the idea.

This whole trip was fruit. Here I was, riding out to the middle of nowhere inside a mirror with a person who looks like me except for prettier eyes, in a car paid for with my future, to a place that gives me the willies. For what? To try and trick her into letting me out of the mirror. The way I was shaking already, things would get reversed and she'd probably be able to talk me into getting my family in here with me.

Enough of this, I thought. There are no aliens, it's an optical illusion, once the car starts rolling uphill she'll be screaming like an honor roll student with her first F and then she'll be mine. I'll play her like a violin. At least like a ukulele.

So then we get there and I run it down the same as Jimmy did to me. Stop the car, Blue Eyes, put it in neutral and turn off the engine. I can't guarantee there are aliens here tonight but if there are we'll know in a minute. They'll start pulling the car up the hill toward their spacecraft. If that happens, remember the magic word. "Louie." Twice. Louie, Louie. Like that oldies song.

All the time I'm setting her up, I can tell she thinks this is all a crock. It wasn't so much what she said; it was more the tears her laughter brought to her eyes.

But then it began to happen. The car moved. Not much at first, about an inch. And then another and then another, still barely moving, but then we went a little faster and then that baby started to roll! I must confess that at the very first movement I gave out a little scream myself, about a thousand decibels worth, but so did Liz. Well, not a scream exactly, but she did quit laughing. For a whole minute. Then she giggled but it was a nervous giggle and I knew I had her.

It was plain she didn't want me to see that she was frightened. Her mouth was moving, saying something, but I couldn't hear her. Then, I did. "Louie, Louie." In a whisper. The car started to pick up more speed. It was hurtling along now at about ten miles per hour.

She said it again—"Louie, Louie"—and this time loud enough to hear plainly. We kept on rolling, the speed now up to a dizzying fifteen miles an hour or so.

"Louie, Louie."

I almost jumped out of my skin *and* the mirror!

"Louie, Louie, Louie, Louie, Louie!"

All right! It was working!

"Liz, listen to me." Here went everything, the whole ball game. Bottom of the ninth, two outs, score tied, me at bat. "You must have the wrong voice tone or something. There's only one way to save us from the aliens." We were halfway "up" the hill now, whipping along at about twenty miles an hour.

"Louie, Louie, Louie, Louie, Louie, *what?*"

"We have to change places. Now. Before we reach the top of the hill. Once we're there, they'll sweep you up into their spaceship. Then it's on to Mars where they breed you with Spider People. Your only chance is to trade places. *Now. Right now.* My voice will work."

There. Now she would have to look at me.

Except she didn't.

CHAPTER TWENTY

She was leaning out of the window and singing. "Louie, Louie" was the song. By the Kingsmen. My dad's favorite song. And she was laughing.

"You didn't think I'd really fall for that weak stuff, did you?"

I considered the next twenty years or so as a mirror person.

"I know all about Gravity Hill, dummy. I was at your pajama party the night after you went the first time. I was in your bedroom mirror."

She started hooting again.

She was fruit. Just plain fruit.

CHAPTER TWENTY-ONE

I must have whizzed in and out of ten mirrors before I ended up at Joe's Gas. It was late, after eleven o'clock. I'd gone home directly from Gravity Hill. *Calamity* Hill was more like it. Party time for Miss Blue Eyes; disaster time for the twin on the inside. It's wrong to hate people maybe, but it was the only enjoyment I was having at the moment.

The situation was hopeless. My fail-proof plan had gone south. With wings. My life was canceled for this season on the boob tube of existence, and any future seasons, thanks to Miss Blue Eyes. I guess I should quit calling her that. Miss Blue Eyes, that is. I was the one with the blue jobs now, and she was sporting the brown numbers. Big deal. I'd give a trillion dollars to have my plain brown ones back again. I knew one thing—if by some miracle I ever got out of here, I'd never wish for a different eye color again. I wouldn't even consider colored contacts. Or red hair or whiter teeth or anything other than what I was shipped with from the factory. Well, maybe I wouldn't be *entirely* and deliriously ecstatic over the teenaged curse of acne, but I'd still trade having jumbo zits from head to toe for being out of here.

I was so bummed at what had happened at Gravity Hill that I'd completely forgotten Mirror Jim's plan. Somehow, my mind had blanked it out, like intense sunspot activity on Channel 10. I just felt so sorry for myself that I sulked in the mirror at Joe's, my head in my hands, invisible to everyone except Miss Blue Eyes, who was gosh-knows-where by now, probably destroying the little bit of my life that was still intact.

Junior was there with one of his slimy buddies, Wimp Belvedere, and they were telling each other jokes, the kind that require an I.Q. that matched the average number of fingers on the average hand. One day soon, Junior and Wimp would end up cellmates, I figured. I was sort of eavesdropping, but my heart really wasn't in it. This was going to be my life from now on, sitting on the sidelines of reality, listening to other people's adventures and never having any to call my own.

Wimp was talking. About me. Natch. Everybody in town was talking about me. I was the center of attention in ways I never dreamed possible. I'd achieved a popularity beyond my wildest nightmares. Wimp was saying, "Yeah, I knew her when she was in the Pom-Pom Club. Really cute. Who would have ever thought she'd turn out this way? I almost took her out one time."

Oh, really. This was news to me. Think again, weasel-face. You must be thinking of someone who looks like me but is more closely related to the Marquis de Sade or is heavily into self-abuse of the third kind. That earthworm had some nerve! Once, I said "hi" to Wimp in passing and almost immediately afterward realized I'd erred on the side of gross dumbness. That was the only communication we'd ever had.

"I remember when she was a pom-pom girl." This was Junior. Somehow, I just knew what he was going to say next and he didn't disappoint me. "She was a pom-pom girl at the game where I broke my leg. That was on the play where Jerry Lerendet ran ninety-six yards. Remember that? Longest run from scrimmage in county history!"

Give it a vacation, Junior! If I hear about your broken leg one more time or Lerendet's run or the block you threw, I'm going to throw up nickels. One for every time you've brought this up in conversation—say about a million bucks' worth. I'll be barfing nickels for a month, and when I'm done I can retire to the Bahamas on a permanent income of nine million bags of small change.

"He does go on about his broken leg, doesn't he?"

I jumped about a foot, straight up.

It was Jim. Mirror Jim. Standing right beside me.

CHAPTER TWENTY-TWO

"You scared me, Mist-Man!"

"Sorry. Didn't work, did it?"

"What? Oh, you mean Gravity Hill."

"Yes. It didn't work, did it? I told you so."

Those are the worst words in the English language. "I told you so." I think they make moms and dads learn it before they allow them to become parents. They, in turn, teach it to your siblings so they can torment you with it.

"So what? It might have worked. It *should* have worked. If she hadn't been snooping on me years ago at a pajama party, it *would've* worked!"

I sniffed.

"I suppose you have a better idea."

As a matter of fact, he did, and as soon as I said that, I remembered. Hope sprang up again. In my bosom, or wherever hope springs up.

"Will it really work?"

"Trust me. It can't miss."

He chuckled.

"What's so funny?"

"Oh, nothing. I was just thinking about Junior there."

"What's so funny about him? I mean, *I* know what's funny, or rather, pitiful, but what strikes *you* funny?"

"His living in the past. He should be in here, instead of you. He's a perfect mirror candidate."

"Why on Earth?"

"Because he lives so much in the past. He could always live in the past in here. Break his dumb leg, over and over. Wouldn't that be some fun!"

"I don't understand."

"Time travel, Elizabeth. Don't you know about that?"

CHAPTER TWENTY-THREE

Time travel...

Interesting...

I had to admit this was news to me. Miss Blue Eyes had never mentioned anything about it.

"You really are naive, aren't you? Don't you know you can go anywhere in time as well as anywhere geographically?"

This was a break-into-prime-time news flash.

"You can?"

"Sure. There's a drawback, though."

Figures. There's *always* a drawback. "What's that?" I said.

"Well..." Mirror Jim paused, as if he was deciding how to tell me. It must be *some* drawback. "...sometimes there's a problem with the molecules of your body all arriving at the same time when you go back and forth in time. I remember one time, I wanted to see what Shakespeare looked like so I went to Stratford, England."

"Well? What happened?"

"I got there, all right. It was really neat. They were all dressed just like you'd figure and all, and they had the neatest accents. You know what was wild? Their accents weren't English at all. They sounded more like they were from North Carolina or something. Weird."

"Yeah, that's weird all right, but WHAT HAPPENED!" Get to the point, Jim-O.

"Well, like I said, I got there, in merry old England, but not all of me. Not right away."

"What do you mean?"

"I mean, all of me got there except for my left foot. My left foot was missing. It must have taken a wrong turn across the ages or something."

I looked at him. Carefully.

"But you have both your feet here." He did, too.

"Oh, it got there. About an hour later. That's the drawback. It all seems to get there, your body, I mean, but sometimes not all at once. It's happened to others in here. All of you gets there, but sometimes not at the same time. Sometimes you have to wait on body parts. Actually, it seems to have to do with the distance you travel. In time. Short trips don't seem to have the same effect. If I went back a couple of years, all I might have to wait on is a finger, say. Maybe a couple of minutes."

I had been getting an idea when Jim first told me about time travel, but that cooked that idea, at least put it on the back burner. I returned to the subject at hand. I'd think about my idea later.

"This great plan of yours you keep talking about, Jim. About tricking Miss Blue—Liz—back into here and me out there. How do I find a mirror like that?"

What I was talking about was Jim's plan. Like I said before, it was so simple and obvious I don't know why I hadn't thought of it myself.

All I had to do was get her to look into a mirror she didn't realize was a mirror. Just long enough for me to say the phrase that would set me free.

And what kind of mirror was that? The kind that had been painted over, for example. I hadn't realized it, before Jim explained it to me, that there were some people who used mirrors for a canvas. Kind of a novelty thing. Sounds like something shut-ins who couldn't get to the mall would end up do-ing. What was good for my predicament was that some of the paintings left just a bit of the mirror uncovered with pigment. Sometimes just a speck or two would be left bare. All I would have to do would be to get Miss Blue Eyes to stare at one of those paintings long enough for me to say my five little words. She wouldn't realize it was a mirror or that I was looking into her eyes until it was too late.

That was the plan.

There was something else Jim had brought up. Once we were switched, another problem arose. How to keep her there. Even if I was successful at trading places back, I would forever have to be on my guard lest I gazed too long into my reflection and she switched us back again. I would always have to sweat that possibility, and I knew she would always be there, watching and waiting for her chance. Talk about a lifetime paranoia!

There was a simple solution to that, too, Jim explained. I only had to get her into a six-sided mirror, a "box" mirror, and then somehow quickly paint all six sides with black paint before she fled to another mirror and safety…and she would be forever imprisoned in that mirror. Jim would help with that, he said, by diverting her attention while I painted the mirror. Then, he would be with the girl of his dreams forever, even though they couldn't see each other. Just two happy mole-mirror-people, was the way he saw it. I could see the beauty of that. If I never saw her face again, it would make *me* deliriously happy. I think Jim looked at that differently. Like it was a small sacrifice he'd be making to be with the girl of his dreams, although that's the kind of dream I'd put in the nightmare category. So far, he seemed like a decent enough guy, so I tried not to think of the horror he was setting himself up for. Being locked up forever in a dark box with Miss Blue Eyes was not my idea of wedded bliss. Ol' Jim, though, was convinced that once she was back inside her mirror world she would become the sweet girl he had once known. I hoped he wouldn't get a smart-attack before we could achieve our goal.

The problem now was twofold. First, to find a

painted mirror, and second, to get her to wherever it was so she would look at it.

Good ol' Jim knew where such a mirror was. Actually, he said he knew where several such mirrors were, but she had already looked at the one he had in mind. Naturally, I hadn't been there; I was probably off at Junior's or somewhere, but according to Jim, she had been where this mirror was located several times and most likely would be there again soon.

The mirror was behind a painting of dogs. It was in Derek Whistler's basement. That was the bad part. Derek was a dropout from Grover Cleveland and a general bum. Derek was the kind of guy that wherever he was standing automatically became the bad part of town. The gossip was that not only did he do drugs, he sold them also. In general, the kind of guy you want to cross the street to avoid. Nobody decent would have anything to do with him. Miss Blue Eyes did, of course. According to Jim, she'd been to his house several times, to parties, smoking grass. That was beautiful. Not only had she destroyed my grades, my relationships, my college education, now she was trashing my brain cells and chromosomes and taking a chance of screwing up my future children. Not to mention taking a chance on mangling my body in a car wreck every time she was high. Lovely girl.

Jim had been spying on her and knew she was due to be at a party tomorrow night at Derek's.

"Eight o'clock, that's when it starts."

"Oh, Jim, this has got to work. If it doesn't work, what am I going to do?"

"It'll work, Elizabeth. And I'll be there with you. Don't worry."

Don't worry! My whole life was riding on his plan.

We made plans to meet at Derek's. Jim started to leave when something he'd said earlier crossed my mind.

"Jim, you said something about time travel. Can I really do that? Tell me how. I want to know exactly how you do that."

CHAPTER TWENTY-FOUR

The next day, the hours sped by like a turtle on Prozac. Kind of like the last day of school. I had now been inside mirrors for three weeks. It felt more like thirty years. Finally, it was seven-thirty, the time I was to meet Jim. In Derek's basement. We wanted to get there before anyone else, just in case Miss Blue Eyes decided to come early. I wasn't about to miss whatever chance I had.

There were just two little paintless specks in the mirror. Whoever painted the picture hadn't meant to leave them; it was an accident. Luck was on my side. They were just the right distance apart for my eyes and they were in a strategic place, in the center of one of the dog's eyes. Right where a viewer's own eyes would be drawn. Jim figured the artist had meant to paint them in and somehow had forgotten. Probably got distracted when the Lawrence Welk show came on. Lucky for me. Thanks, Lawrence.

We could see Derek coming and going. He was

doing things like bringing down bags of ice to the refrigerator and setting out bottles of booze. From where we were, we could only see part of the room. It was a dumpy basement. The wall opposite us was paneled with this stuff they used a thousand years ago, and there were several holes in the paneling. Fists, Jim said. Drunk kids punching holes. I hope they broke a few knuckles, I thought. Nice parties. Nice folks. Like from the right distance, Cujo probably looked like a nice doggie.

People began arriving. Sort of the cast for a movie to be called "Scum People With Unsuccessful Lobotomies." Not a one in the bunch I'd want to share a cab with. So these are Miss Blue Eyes's new friends. *My* friends, as far as the world was concerned.

I began wondering if getting back to the real world would be worth it. I was going to have such a reputation when I got out. It would take the biggest P.R. campaign in the history of politics, just to get my image back up to the level of Typhoid Mary.

It was now eight-thirty and the party was in full swing, but still no Liz. I was beginning to worry but Jim calmed me down. "She's learned a tactic called 'being fashionably late,'" he said. "She does it all the time. Don't worry, she'll be here."

Sure. Easy for you to say, Jim. You're safe at home with nothing to worry about. Me, I'm this ghost with a zero future, with this insane person running around going potty on my rep.

What a party! A bunch of pea-brains sitting

around using their twelve-word vocabularies, prefacing each sentence with, "like, yeah, man," and whiz-kid stuff like that, and smoking dope and chugging beer. They really thought they were "with it" and what they were, mostly, was pathetic. I recognized a couple of kids I realized I hadn't seen in a while. They'd dropped out of life, at least school life, and now I saw why. They were all zombie-heads. That's our term for dopers. I felt sorry for them. Some of them had been pretty good kids, but here they were at Derek's, performing major brain and body damage to their earthly units.

Liz came in!

CHAPTER TWENTY-FIVE

Everybody seemed to know her, which cut another chunk out of my self-esteem. I heard two sleazeball boys sitting on the moldy couch just beneath the mirror Jim and I were in say something about "Easy Liz" when she walked in. If I wasn't already on Cloud Nine, that sure did it. I put my hands over my ears so I wouldn't have to hear any more. It didn't do any good, as loud as their voices were. They discussed what a jerk she was, snickering as they made scintillating comments about her character. Or, rather, lack of any. A plus, in their eyes. Kind of a Siskel and Ebert of the Sewer Set. Two thumbs up for the tramp. I wished she could hear how her "friends" talked about her. One of them yelled at her and she came over and you'd never know they'd ever said anything bad about her in the way they greeted her.

"Hi, Liz, how's my favorite mama!"
and,

"Hey, Babe, yer lookin' good!"

Barftime. Their lines weren't any more original than the oily jeans they were wearing. Liz, on the other hand, ate it up. You could see by her expression she thought these morons were great thinkers or Jonathan Taylor Thomas or something. I wanted to yank her hair out. She was destroying my reputation for intelligence by even breathing the same air as these slugs.

Look at the picture, I screamed inside, wishing with all my might. *Look at me!*

My heart leaped up close to where my tonsils used to be when she glanced up at the dog for a second, and my mouth opened to speak, but all I got out was "I want" before she glanced away.

"Be patient," said Jim, standing at my elbow. "You'll have your chance."

My spirits went in the same direction as the Titanic when she turned and walked over to the other side of the room where a group of people were passing around a joint.

"Don't put that stuff in my body!" I screamed, but naturally she didn't hear. Which in a way was good, since it didn't alert her as to where I was hiding.

"Let her go," said Jim. "You want her to get stoned."

"I do?" I answered. "Why?"

"'Cause. Then she'll be so spaced she'll probably stare at the picture for hours. You'll be able to say what you have to at seventy-eight rpm or a word a week. Just watch and see."

Easy for Jim to say. He wasn't the one with everything on the line. Then I thought, I'm not being fair to him. He's been a really nice guy and if it wasn't for him I wouldn't even be here and might never have thought of this scheme. I smiled at him, feeling contrite.

"It's okay, Elizabeth. You have a right to feel like you do. Just don't be so hard on Liz. She just doesn't know how to handle all this freedom all at once. Once she's back in here she'll change back to the sweet Liz I love."

Yes, and gerbils will rule the White House on Thursday. I'd forgotten his mind-reading abilities. I felt warm with shame. He *was* a nice guy, a lot like my own Jimmy. I hoped he was right about her, for his own sake. Wouldn't it be horrible to be trapped forever in a mirror with a cretin, like she was now?

For the next two hours, Liz wandered around the room, smoking dope, guzzling beer, kissing this boy and then that one, and in general, acting like the queen of sluts. Once in a while, she'd glance our way, but never long enough for me to say what I had to. I was going Looney Tunes. She was never going to look at the picture long enough.

Then people started leaving. The dope must be all gone, I thought. There was certainly no other reason for them to stay. Why else would anyone want to be around kids like this, unless they could leech drugs off of them? Except for that misery loving company thing, that is. Or birds of a feather flocking together. Or bird-brains. I certainly didn't know anyone with a modicum of "cool" who would be caught dead here.

It wasn't going to work. There Miss Blue Eyes went for the pile of coats. She found hers and put it on. My life was over.

She waved goodbye to those who could half understand her and then started up the stairs. Her head had already disappeared and all that was visible were her legs when one of the slimeballs on the couch beneath us screeched out, "Hey, Liz, wait a minute!"

One leg disappeared out of sight and then the other. She hadn't heard him. I groaned and got ready to leave myself, my heart broken and ready to be tossed in the dumpster. I'll go to Junior's, I thought. It's depressing, but not as sad as here with these Cro-Magnons. And then, just as I was getting ready to mirrorport, her foot came back into view. I knew it was her foot because she had on my Agner pumps I had saved sixty years for. She'd already scuffed them up.

It *was* her. She was just running on delayed-reaction time. She came back down the stairs, part-way, and leaned over the railing, squinting at the bozos on the couch.

"Whadya want?" she hissed.

"I didn't get a kiss," said Turniphead. It was a name I'd given him earlier. His partner I'd been thinking of as Pus Brains. Pus Brains mumbled something about not getting one either. A kiss.

Don't do it, I thought. I'd rather stay in here a million years than have someone see me kiss one of these cruds.

So, of course she had to come over to them. I needed something for my stomach. Like ten gallons of Pepto-Bismol. Jim brought me back to reality.

"Now's your chance," he said softly.

CHAPTER TWENTY-SIX

He was right. There she was, not two feet away, facing us. But not looking up. One of the slugs on the couch handed her the joint they had been sharing. She took it and puffed, squinting her eyes like it was a lemon. She looked at the dog. At me.

"I want to…"

She looked back down, passed the roach back to one of the zeros. Rats!

"Well, I gotta be splittin'," she said, turning.

"One more toke," said Pus Brains.

She turned back, shrugging her shoulders.

"One more."

She accepted the joint and put it to her lips, pursing them and looking incredibly ugly.

But beautiful. Because her eyes were directly on mine.

"I want to trade places!"

I said it quick and her eyes were on me the whole while. But nothing happened. Not a darned thing.

Tears began to well up in my eyes as all hope drained from me. I handed the joint back to one of the boys and started to walk away; I took two or three steps before it hit me.

CHAPTER TWENTY-SEVEN

I was out. Out of the mirror. And in the last place on earth I would ever want to be. I started moving my legs toward the stairs.

"Hey, Liz," came a voice from behind me. It was Turniphead. "What about my kiss?"

I turned and faced him, very carefully avoiding the painting that hung above the couch.

"My name is Elizabeth," I said, enunciating each word clearly. "And I wouldn't kiss you, you slug—" I paused to give each word so they would penetrate his dim-bulbed head, "—if you were to promise me a million dollars for doing so. In fact," I paused again, "I'm going straight home and shower for about six hours and then spend the next two days brushing my teeth. I don't think the scum will come off even then, but I'm going to try."

The room quieted. Everybody was staring at me like I had green hair. I take that back. If I'd only had green hair, nobody in *that* room would've given me a second glance.

I looked around at Derek and the others who were still there. "If any of you dimwits ever even pretends like you know me, I'll call the police on you. Or better yet, the dog pound. Don't any of you ever come near me again. Ever."

I stalked up the stairs. No one breathed behind me.

I found my college education and drove it home. I was manic-depressive—ecstatic over being out of the mirror and suicidal at the thought of how my life had been trashed.

I started getting a glimpse of the way things were as soon as I returned home.

"Hi, Mom," I said when I walked through the door. She and Dad were sitting in the living room, reading. "Hi, Daddy."

Neither even looked up. I couldn't blame them, I guess. Be brave, I told myself. Time is on your side. Eventually, they'll see you're their sweet, lovable Elizabeth again. Like in about seventy-five years, maybe. I decided not to press it. I went into the kitchen. Mikey was there.

"Hi, Mikey," I said, a smile on my lips. "Wanna play some checkers?"

Mikey looked up at me and his eyes showed white. "Don't hit me, Liz. I'll do anything you want."

I couldn't help it. I sat down on a kitchen chair and buried my head in my arms on the table, not even trying to hold back the waterworks. Everyone hated and feared me. All of the time in the world couldn't fix this or heal it. Miss Blue Eyes had certainly done a thorough job of spoiling my life. I heard Mikey patter around behind me and the kitchen door squeaked as he burst through it. He was sneaking out, scared to death of me.

This should be the happiest day of my life; instead it's the worst. I suddenly couldn't even cry. I was so sad the tears wouldn't come. I lifted my head and found myself staring right into the kitchen mirror.

And there she was.

Liz.

CHAPTER TWENTY-EIGHT

She was mad.

I looked away quickly. It might be bad out here, but there was no way I was ever going back in there. At least if I was out here I could begin rebuilding my life. Even though it was going to take an architect with the skills of Frank Lloyd Wright and the brain of Einstein.

That reminded me of what I had to do. I had to make sure she stayed in that mirror. Forever.

I got up and went back out to the living room. Mom and Dad were still there, pretending to be reading but I could tell they were watching me out of the corners of their eyes. Mikey was there, too, sitting right next to Dad. For protection, I guessed.

I walked right by them and outside. Inside, I was experiencing the world's biggest broken heart but I couldn't let that stop me. I had to do what had to be done. I had to lock Liz up, once and for all.

Then I could start putting the pieces of my life back together.

I got to the drugstore just as it was closing. All the way there I studiously avoided looking into the car mirror. Once inside the drugstore I located what I needed, took it to the checkout counter and paid for it. I drove straight home, resisting the urge to speed. I wanted this over with.

Back home I went straight inside, through the living room where my family still sat as they had when I left, and downstairs to the basement. I went over to Dad's workbench and emptied the large bag from the drugstore. It was all there. Paint, six mirrors and Super Glue. I worked as fast as I could, gluing the mirrors together until I had a box, mirrors on all sides. I was careful not to look into any of the mirrors for more than a second or two at a time. I took the gallon of black paint, and using a screwdriver, got the lid off.

Then I sat down on the stool before the workbench and picked up the mirror box and held it above the gallon of paint. And waited.

She didn't take long. Maybe five minutes.

"Let me out!" she screamed.

I became the Cheshire Cat in Alice in Wonderland.

"I don't think so, cookie."

"Let me out and I'll let you trade back any time you want." Her voice became wheedling, conciliatory. I glanced into the mirror and saw myself. With blue eyes. I got just a glimpse of them before I concentrated on staring at my chin. I had learned well. I let her rant and rave and plead for as long as she wanted. I was enjoying this. Revenge *was* sweet. I was just waiting for something. A second later, what I was waiting for happened.

CHAPTER TWENTY-NINE

"Hi, Liz." It was Jim. He was in there with her. Perfect! Just what I was waiting for. I did it.

I just let the mirror fall. Into the bucket of black paint. And I nailed her. In the split second before the paint covered the top I heard her screaming, "Oh, no. No, no, no." And then she was gone. I had her. Locked away for eternity.

I took one last look at the paint can before I left. I'd replaced the lid and shoved it to the back of the bench. Tomorrow I'd take the bucket and hide it where no one would ever find it. Somewhere safe where the mirror couldn't ever be broken and release her.

I went back up the stairs and turned off the light. Now to work on getting my life back together.

As I passed the hall mirror, I took a quick glance at myself. Brown eyes. Beautiful brown eyes.

I grinned at myself and headed into the living room where I sat down and pretended to read part of the paper. My family was still there but they didn't acknowledge me. It wouldn't work to rush things, I figured. Just take it one day at a time until they saw I was the old Elizabeth. I had realized I couldn't rebuild Rome in one day.

CHAPTER THIRTY

School was a joyride through Bluebird Heaven. My friends (make that *former* friends) looked at me like their shoes were too tight, while the unsavory element welcomed me with the same glee the local undertaker must have when introduced to each of Henry the Eighth's new wives.

It was the longest day I can ever remember. At noon, I went into the bathroom where my group always went, and the reception was so frosty I felt like rubbing snow on my nose to get the circulation going again.

I paid no attention to any of it. I was determined to smile, smile, and then smile some more, and in general act so sweet that cavities would act up when I walked by. By the time the last bell had rung for the day, my face had freeze-dried into a perma-nent smirk and was beginning to crinkle into tiny porcelain pieces. My heart had already crinkled.

I saw Jimmy in first-hour algebra. That was sure

some fun. I said a cheery "hi" to him and he gave me an equally cheery "drop dead." My plan was obviously working. By the time I rounded my first century of existence, we would once again be on a first-name basis.

Somehow, I got through the bliss-filled day and headed home. Walking. I'd never see the inside of Jimmy French's car again, that seemed certain. When I passed by Mrs. Brown's interior decorating shop on Oak Street, I couldn't help it. I glanced in. Sure enough, she had her usual mirror display up. I had avoided mirrors all day. No reason, I knew, just force of habit. This was the first one. I just gave it a fast peek and walked on. Halfway down the block it hit me and my knees buckled. I had blue eyes.

Liz was out!

She'd escaped, somehow!

No! That's impossible. I must have imagined it. There's no way she could have gotten free. She's at home, in a six-sided mirror sitting in a bucket of black paint. It's just nerves, I kept insisting to myself. Just dumb old nerves. I need a vacation. Some distant country where, if they saw a mirror they'd think it was from their demon god.

Nevertheless, I used my Olympic walk the rest of the way home. Once I got there, I burst through the front door and headed straight for the basement. Dad intercepted me before I could reach the door that led downstairs.

"Liz!"

I turned to face him. This was the first he'd spoken to me since I'd been back. He wouldn't look directly at me, like he thought I was going to sass him or embarrass him.

"Liz, would you mind helping your mother a minute?"

"Of course, Dad. Where is she? And, Dad, would you please call me Elizabeth?"

He looked at me like he was amazed that my head hadn't started spinning and barfing green pea soup. Poor Daddy! He looked so forlorn! I hated Miss Blue Eyes more than ever for doing this to my family.

"Your mom's upstairs. In the bathroom. Trying to wash off Mikey."

I turned and started for the stairs, my heart fluttering around in my mouth like a bat caught outside his cave at dawn. I went up the stairs, two at a time. Behind me, I heard my father.

"Mikey got into some paint. It's all over him. Ask Mother if she needs any more towels. I'm going to clean up the basement. There's paint all over and it looks like glass as well. Your brother!"

CHAPTER THIRTY-ONE

I saw two things at the same time. Mom bending over Mikey in the bathtub, black everywhere and Miss Blue Eyes leering out of the mirror at me. It was stacking up to be a banner day.

"Let me help, Mom," I said. First things first. Get Mikey cleaned up. I couldn't even get mad at him. I was just so glad to be back out here with him that I didn't care that he had loosed the demon.

"Get Liz out of here!" he screamed when he saw me. "She's gonna hit me and I don't want her to see me neked." He said it like that—"neked."

"Mikey," I said, walking over to the tub and picking up a washcloth. "You're six and a half and have at least another year to go before you're allowed to be modest."

I looked up at the mirror. She was still there. I was careful to not look at her eyes for more than a second.

"I'll take care of you soon," I said to the mirror.

"What?" said Mom. Mikey just screamed something unintelligible as I reached for his arm.

"Nothing, Mom. Here, you hold one arm and I'll hold the other and you hose him down."

Together, we got the worst of it off of him. Luckily, I had purchased water-based paint. We got all of it off except for his hair. His blond hair was now the color Elvis favored. Mom and I both laughed at the sight. Mikey wasn't too thrilled at the change in his appearance, but the age of six is a wondrous cure for problems of this sort. Sixty seconds later he was interested in something else, some rediscovered toy, and he was off and playing with it, unaware of his uncanny resemblance to a dead rock-and-roll hero.

We were still laughing when he ran out of the bathroom, and Mom turned and caught my eye with a chuckle still in her throat. It died there, as he cleared it out, harrumphing in seeming embarrassment.

"Thanks, Liz," she said softly, and then bent to gather up the towels and washrags.

"Mom, I—" I didn't know what to say. She'd never in a hundred years believe what had happened and trying to explain would only make it worse. I clammed my lips shut. She stood up and opened her mouth as if to say something further and then kind of shook her head a little, turned and left the room, leaving me sitting on the floor.

I knew what I was going to have to do. It was

plain as a Friday night pimple that I was never going to undo the damage Miss Blue Eyes had wrought upon my once peaceful existence. Without knowing it, Jim, Liz's Jim, had shown me what had to be done. It was something he had once said. About Junior. When he had talked about the past and how Junior would be at home in the mirror since he could always live in the past.

That was when he'd told me about time travel and explained how to do it. It was easy. Or so it sounded. I hadn't tried it, but I had no reason to believe it wasn't exactly as he had said. Somehow, I knew that Jim never lied, and somehow, I knew that he had told me about the phenomenon for a reason. This reason.

There was only one tiny drawback. Time travel could only be achieved in Mirror World. And there was that other little snag. You might end up without your entire body unit, at first.

I had to do it. There was no other choice. My life was ruined unless I could go back to that moment when I had traded places with Miss Blue Eyes and reverse my decision. I would be on the opposite side of the mirror this time and the farthest I could go back would be to the exact second I entered the mirror. But something had happened at that moment that told me my plan would work. Miss Blue Eyes had stared at me for nearly a full minute, gloating, before she turned and ran out of the bathroom. I was counting on her exhibiting the same obnoxious

behavior in the same way, once again.
That was it. I was going back into the mirror.
On purpose.
Ohboyohboyohboy...

CHAPTER THIRTY-TWO

My hands were sweating and my mind churned over what I needed to do and how to accomplish it. By going back to that exact moment, I would have time to shout the words out before she averted her gaze. And, I would be out again, back in my own world before she had the opportunity to do anything to wreck my life.

The only thing that could go wrong would be that she wouldn't stand and stare in triumph at me like she had the first time, but instead flee the bathroom immediately. If that happened, I'd be trapped for good, since it was unlikely she'd ever place herself in a position to be tricked again. It was a chance I had to take. I wanted my life back. I wanted my family back. I wanted Jimmy back.

I was betting that she would remain true to her nature.

If all went well the whole thing would take less than an hour.

I'd be back in time for supper. If I remembered right, three weeks ago Mom had planned roast beef for that night. My favorite.

I knew I'd have an appetite, regardless of all the chocolate chip cookies I'd inhaled.

I stood up.

I walked to the bathroom.

I took a deep breath.

I looked into the mirror and deep into my eyes.

They were blue.

CHAPTER THIRTY-THREE

It was horrible at first. I was back in the mirror—*of my own volition—don't tell me how crazy that was!*—and I wasn't even sure time travel actually worked.

It had to. It just had to!

I found myself in the mirror at Derek's. Behind the dog painting. Mirror Jim was there, too. At first, I just stood there and stared out. I thought I could see someone's feet disappearing up the stairs. Whoever it was had on my shoes. There wasn't anybody else there, but the place was a mess. I looked at Jim and could barely keep myself from crying.

"It's two days later," Jim said. I'd forgotten he could read my mind.

"She just came by to pick up a sweater."

So those were *my* shoes! And my nemesis.

"You just had to come back, didn't you?" he said, his eyes sad. "How do you think you're going to get back out now? Liz is going to be a hundred times harder to trick now." He shook his head, like he was supremely disgusted. I guess I knew how he felt. Here he had his girlfriend back and then I'd done this.

"Jim…" I explained to him why I'd come back.

"It *might* work," he said, but he sounded unsure.

"It *has* to work," I said. "You told me time travel was easy."

"I did, didn't I," he said. "Well, it is," he went on. "For me. But then…I've been doing it all my life. I've got lots of practice. You've never done it before."

"I learn quick," I said. "Especially if I concentrate and focus." And boy! Was I focused!

"Okay," he said. "Give it a stab."

I did what he'd told me you had to do. Closed my eyes, picked out the spot I wanted to arrive at and the time—the *exact* time—that was crucial—and simply wished.

I could feel something happening to my body, something indescribable. I hadn't thought you could feel anything in here, nothing physical that is, but there was something very physical happening to me. It felt like…what? The closest I can come to describing the experience is that it felt like swimming in Jell-O. Not that I've ever swam in Jell-O. It just felt like what I imagine that would be like.

When the feeling stopped and I felt normal again, I still kept my eyes closed. I was so afraid I'd still be standing there with Jim, in the picture in Derek's basement. If I opened my eyes and he was there I was going to die. I might as well.

Finally, I opened my eyes, first one, just squinting a little and then the other, and then I opened them wide.

CHAPTER THIRTY-FOUR

Success!

I was in the bathroom mirror. And at the right time. I knew it was the right time because there were Mom's pink towels right in front of me. Ever since Liz and I had traded the first time, she'd been putting the yellow ones in the bathroom. And Liz was standing there, looking in the mirror, a smirk on her face. I remembered that smirk. It was the same one she'd worn right after we'd traded places the very first time.

I looked down at my feet. Hooray! They were both there! I'd arrived in one piece!

Or had I? I checked my other body parts, my legs, my arms and hands. My hands! My right one was there, but my left one...my left one was missing. My left arm ended at my wrist. Oh, my gosh...

Liz was saying something. "Yes, Elizabeth, and your eyes are blue now. Didn't..."

This was the time! I had just a few seconds to say the magic words and reverse everything that had happened. But I couldn't go back out missing a hand!

"…you always…" At the end of this sentence I had to make my move. I had to make a decision. I brought my left arm up. It was coming back! I could just see a ghostly outline, not the whole hand, but it was reappearing. I had to go, hand or not. I had to say the magic words *right now.* I could only hope the rest of my hand would appear in time.

CHAPTER THIRTY-FIVE

"…want blue eyes?"

I just stared at her.
I had to say the words.
I couldn't.
I was frozen.
I opened my mouth.
Nothing came out.
Then…

CHAPTER THIRTY-SIX

"I...I..."

I was stuttering!
 I gulped air back, made my mind go blank.
 Spoke.
 "Iwanttotradeplaces." I said it *fast*. No, I said it
with the speed of light.

CHAPTER THIRTY-SEVEN

And I was out.

I looked at Liz, trapped inside the mirror and a look of shock and surprise passed over her face and then her features scrunched up into a look of absolute rage and she started to say, "I want…" I slammed my eyes shut and turned away quickly.

I heard Mom come in the front door and call my name. "Elizabeth! Where are you, hon?"

I felt like crying, I was so happy.

"I'm coming, Mom. Be there in a minute."

Then I did the hardest thing I've ever had to do. I forced myself to look at my left hand.

It was there! Only…something was missing. At first, I didn't know what was wrong. All my fingers were there. And then I saw. I was missing a fingernail! Just one. My index finger. The complete nail was gone. In the mirror someplace, I guessed. Floating around. My finger didn't hurt or anything. It was just missing a nail.

I could live with that.

"Bye, Blue Eyes," I said, glancing briefly at my twin. She was scowling. I caught a glimpse of Jim standing behind her. He was smiling.

So was I.

CHAPTER THIRTY-EIGHT

It's been three months now and everything's fine. My fingernail has even grown back, only it's not the same as it used to be. It's turned a kind of pale silvery color. Weird!

Other than that, it's almost as if the whole thing never happened. Almost…The rest of it went pretty much the way I'd hoped and planned. I was able to get her back into a six-sided mirror again—since we'd gone back in time she hadn't remembered how I'd tricked her before—and *this* time, I took the bucket of paint out right away and buried it deep. Very deep. In the woods alongside Gravity Hill. That sure brought back some memories!

At the time I buried her, I figured I'd be safe for always, but I heard Dad say something disturbing the other day. Something about a new housing project scheduled for out by the airport. Out by Gravity Hill. I don't know if it's in the same place where I buried the bucket, but I'm going to find out. If it is,

I'll just dig her up and bury her again. If I have to keep moving her the rest of my life, well, then I'll just do it. It's a small price to pay for my freedom.

Lots of great things are happening. Jimmy surprised me with the nicest ring. It's a pre-engagement ring, with an opal, my favorite stone. We've decided we won't even think about marriage until we both get out of college, but that won't take that long. A measly four years. Well, for me, anyway. The way Jimmy studies, it could take him six, but I figure I'll help him all I can and get him through on time. No way I'm waiting six years to become Mrs. Elizabeth French. That boy's fate is sealed.

I got accepted at Indiana University. The letter came last week. Our whole family went out and celebrated over in Fort Wayne, at this really great restaurant that has the best onion rings. They call it an "onion loaf" and it looks just like a loaf of homemade bread when they serve it. The only thing that tastes better in the entire universe is the perfect pizza, the way they do it at Oley's Pizza.

I'm going to study English and folklore. That way I can write stories about all those things I've suddenly gotten interested in. You know, elves and fairies and gremlins. And Mirror People. I want to tell their story. Maybe there are others who've had the same experience I have. I want to tell Mirror Jim's story. And Betty's, from Fairmont. When I look back on it, there are some awfully nice people trapped inside mirrors. I have this idea that the more I study folklore and the more I learn, I may discover a way to help them escape, come out into the real world. Even Liz. Maybe if she had a true friend, she'd change, become a regular person.

That's all a long way off. First, I have to study for my finals or there won't be any college, and I definitely don't want to end up at the age of sixty with a name tag over my shirt pocket, pressing a spatula down on a greasy burger. I still remember my dream about Jimmy!

That reminds me. I have to find a dress for the prom. And yes, I'm going with Jimmy. The only problem is, he wants to double with Susie White and her new boyfriend. It turns out Susie's started dating Junior. You know, Joe's boy, who runs the gas station? If he so much as *begins* his story about his stupid football block, I'm going to break his other leg.

I mean it. Or, I may just play a little prank on him. I may just have him stare into the mirror and say this little phrase I picked up. Five little words. Who knows? He may have his own mirror twin. We may just find out.

Wouldn't that be *sweet*!

ACKNOWLEDGMENTS

A big thank-you as always to my wife Mary, who grows more beautiful every day and is the perfect writer's wife. To one terrific publisher, Eric Campbell and his henchman, Lance Wright. And a big shout-out to the cover designer, J.T. Lindroos who is just one of the very best in the business.

LES EDGERTON is an ex-con, matriculating at Pendleton Reformatory in the sixties for burglary. He was an outlaw for many years and was involved in shootouts, knifings, robberies, high-speed car chases, dealt and used drugs, was a pimp, worked for an escort service, starred in porn movies, was a gambler, served four years in the Navy, and had other misadventures. He's since taken a vow of poverty (became a writer) with twenty-one books in print. Work of his has been nominated for or won the Pushcart Prize, O. Henry Award, Edgar Allan Poe Award, Derringer Award, PEN/ Faulkner Award, Jesse Jones Book Award, the Violet Crown Book Award among others. He holds a B.A. from I.U. and an MFA in Writing from Vermont College. He lives in Ft. Wayne, Indiana, where he immigrated to some years ago from the U.S. and is currently learning the language and customs there. He writes because he hates...a lot...and hard. Injustice and bullying are what he hates the most.

LesEdgertonOnWriting.blogspot.com

On the following pages are a few
more great titles from the
Down & Out Books publishing family.

For a complete list of books and to
sign up for our newsletter,
go to DownAndOutBooks.com.

Seven Ways to Get Rid of Harry
Jen Conley

Down & Out Books
June 2019
978-1-948235-93-8

Danny Zelko, needs to get rid of his mom's boyfriend, Harry. The guy is a creep. Of course everyone blames Danny. It's his fault he gets into fights at school. It's his fault he can't control his anger. Danny isn't such a bad kid—he has his own lawn business, makes his own dinner, even takes out the garbage without being asked. All he wants is for his mom to be like she used to be—a real mother who acted like one. Because Harry makes her stupid. And the prospect of spending another day with this man makes Danny feel helpless and broken.

Danny, never the one to cower, decides to do something.

Hipster Death Rattle
Richie Narvaez

Down & Out Books
March 2019
978-1-948235-63-1

Murder is trending. Hipsters are getting slashed to pieces in the hippest neighborhood in New York: Williamsburg, Brooklyn.

While Detectives Petrosino and Hadid hound local gangbangers, slacker reporter Tony Moran and his ex Magaly Fernandez get caught up in a missing person's case—one that might just get them hacked to death.

I'm Not Happy Till You're Not Happy
Crime Stories by Ryan Sayles

All Due Respect, an imprint of
Down & Out Books
978-1-948235-19-8

From a bank robbery gone horribly wrong to a shipwrecked man with a serious anger problem to a lonely teenage Peeping Tom, Ryan Sayles's second collection of stories steam rolls along.

Need a transvestite beating up her drug dealer? Got it. What about a guy trying to stuff a dead hooker into his trunk? Got it also. Need a Richard Dean Buckner story? Got two of 'em.

Come on in and join the mayhem.

Fast Bang Booze
Lawrence Maddox

Shotgun Honey, an imprint of
Down & Out Books
978-1-946502-54-4

After seeing Frank deliver an impressive ass kicking in a bar fight, Russian mobster Popov hires him to be his driver. What Popov doesn't know is that when Frank is sober, he's inhumanly fast, deadly, and mute; when Frank is on the sauce, he's a useless twenty-something wiseass.

Double-crossed in a drug deal gone bad, Frank and Popov have one night to recover their stolen cash or get wiped off the map. Frank's special abilities put him in the spotlight, and he struggles to keep it all together…